T0144353

Ziska

Ziska

Marie Corelli

MINT EDITIONS

Ziska was first published in 1897.

This edition published by Mint Editions 2021.

ISBN 9781513278223 | E-ISBN 9781513278681

Published by Mint Editions®

MINT
EDITIONS
minteditionbooks.com

Publishing Director: Jennifer Newens
Design & Production: Rachel Lopez Metzger
Project Manager: Micaela Clark
Typesetting: Westchester Publishing Services

Contents

PROLOGUE

Dark against the sky towered the Great Pyramid, and over its apex hung the moon. Like a wreck cast ashore by some titanic storm, the Sphinx, reposing amid the undulating waves of grayish sand surrounding it, seemed for once to drowse. Its solemn visage that had impassively watched ages come and go, empires rise and fall, and generations of men live and die, appeared for the moment to have lost its usual expression of speculative wisdom and intense disdain—its cold eyes seemed to droop, its stern mouth almost smiled. The air was calm and sultry; and not a human foot disturbed the silence. But towards midnight a Voice suddenly arose as it were like a wind in the desert, crying aloud: "Araxes! Araxes!" and wailing past, sank with a profound echo into the deep recesses of the vast Egyptian tomb. Moonlight and the Hour wove their own mystery; the mystery of a Shadow and a Shape that flitted out like a thin vapor from the very portals of Death's ancient temple, and drifting forward a few paces resolved itself into the visionary fairness of a Woman's form—a Woman whose dark hair fell about her heavily, like the black remnants of a long-buried corpse's wrappings; a Woman whose eyes flashed with an unholy fire as she lifted her face to the white moon and waved her ghostly arms upon the air. And again the wild Voice pulsated through the stillness.

"Araxes! . . . Araxes! Thou art here,
—and I pursue thee! Through life into
death; through death out into life again!
I find thee and I follow! I follow!
Araxes! . . ."

Moonlight and the Hour wove their own mystery; and ere the pale opal dawn flushed the sky with hues of rose and amber the Shadow had vanished; the Voice was heard no more. Slowly the sun lifted the edge of its golden shield above the horizon, and the great Sphinx awaking from its apparent brief slumber, stared in expressive and eternal scorn across the tracts of sand and tufted palm-trees towards the glittering dome of El-Hazar—that abode of profound sanctity and learning, where men still knelt and worshipped, praying the Unknown to deliver them from the Unseen. And one would almost have deemed that the sculptured Monster with the enigmatical Woman-face and Lion-form had strange thoughts in its huge granite brain; for when the full day sprang in glory over the desert and illumined its large features with a burning saffron radiance, its cruel lips still smiled as though yearning to speak and propound the terrible riddle of old time; the Problem which killed!

I

It was the full "season" in Cairo. The ubiquitous Britisher and the no less ubiquitous American had planted their differing "society" standards on the sandy soil watered by the Nile, and were busily engaged in the work of reducing the city, formerly called Al Kahira or The Victorious, to a more deplorable condition of subjection and slavery than any old-world conqueror could ever have done. For the heavy yoke of modern fashion has been flung on the neck of Al Kahira, and the irresistible, tyrannic dominion of "swagger" vulgarity has laid The Victorious low. The swarthy children of the desert might, and possibly would, be ready and willing to go forth and fight men with men's weapons for the freedom to live and die unmolested in their own native land; but against the blandly-smiling, white-helmeted, sun-spectacled, perspiring horde of Cook's "cheap trippers," what can they do save remain inert and well-nigh speechless? For nothing like the cheap tripper was ever seen in the world till our present enlightened and glorious day of progress; he is a new-grafted type of nomad, like and yet unlike a man. The Darwin theory asserts itself proudly and prominently in bristles of truth all over him—in his restlessness, his ape-like agility and curiosity, his shameless inquisitiveness, his careful cleansing of himself from foreign fleas, his general attention to minutiae, and his always voracious appetite; and where the ape ends and the man begins is somewhat difficult to discover. The "image of God" wherewith he, together with his fellows, was originally supposed to be impressed in the first fresh days of Creation, seems fairly blotted out, for there is no touch of the Divine in his mortal composition. Nor does the second created phase-the copy of the Divineo—namely, the Heroic,—dignify his form or ennoble his countenance. There is nothing of the heroic in the wandering biped who swings through the streets of Cairo in white flannels, laughing at the staid composure of the Arabs, flicking thumb and finger at the patient noses of the small hireable donkeys and other beasts of burden, thrusting a warm red face of inquiry into the shadowy recesses of odoriferous bazaars, and sauntering at evening in the Esbekiyeh Gardens, cigar in mouth and hands in pockets, looking on the scene and behaving in it as if the whole place were but a reflex of Earl's Court Exhibition. History affects the cheap tripper not at all; he regards the Pyramids as "good building" merely, and the inscrutable

Sphinx itself as a fine target for empty soda-water bottles, while perhaps his chiefest regret is that the granite whereof the ancient monster is hewn is too hard for him to inscribe his distinguished name thereon. It is true that there is a punishment inflicted on any person or persons attempting such wanton work—a fine or the bastinado; yet neither fine nor bastinado would affect the "tripper" if he could only succeed in carving "'Arry" on the Sphinx's jaw. But he cannot, and herein is his own misery. Otherwise he comports himself in Egypt as he does at Margate, with no more thought, reflection, or reverence than dignify the composition of his far-off Simian ancestor.

Taking him all in all, he is, however, no worse, and in some respects better, than the "swagger" folk who "do" Egypt, or rather, consent in a languid way to be "done" by Egypt. These are the people who annually leave England on the plea of being unable to stand the cheery, frosty, and in every respect healthy winter of their native country—that winter, which with its wild winds, its sparkling frost and snow, its holly trees bright with scarlet berries, its merry hunters galloping over field and moor during daylight hours, and its great log fires roaring up the chimneys at evening, was sufficiently good for their forefathers to thrive upon and live through contentedly up to a hale and hearty old age in the times when the fever of travelling from place to place was an unknown disease, and home was indeed "sweet home." Infected by strange maladies of the blood and nerves, to which even scientific physicians find it hard to give suitable names, they shudder at the first whiff of cold, and filling huge trunks with a thousand foolish things which have, through luxurious habit, become necessities to their pallid existences, they hastily depart to the Land of the Sun, carrying with them their nameless languors, discontents and incurable illnesses, for which Heaven itself, much less Egypt, could provide no remedy. It is not at all to be wondered at that these physically and morally sick tribes of human kind have ceased to give any serious attention as to what may possibly become of them after death, or whether there Is any "after," for they are in the mentally comatose condition which precedes entire wreckage of brain-force; existence itself has become a "bore;" one place is like another, and they repeat the same monotonous round of living in every spot where they congregate, whether it be east, west, north, or south. On the Riviera they find little to do except meet at Rumpelmayer's at Cannes, the London House at Nice, or the Casino at Monte-Carlo; and in Cairo they inaugurate a miniature London "season" over again, worked in the same groove of dinners, dances, drives, picnics, flirtations, and matrimonial engagements. But the Cairene season has perhaps some advantage over the London one so far as this particular set of "swagger" folk are concerned—it is less hampered by the proprieties. One can be more "free," you know! You may take a little walk into "Old" Cairo, and turning a corner you may catch glimpses of what Mark Twain calls "Oriental simplicity," namely, picturesquely-composed groups of "dear delightful" Arabs whose clothing is no more than primitive custom makes strictly necessary. These kind of "tableaux vivants" or "art studies" give quite a thrill of novelty to Cairene-English Society,—a touch of savagery,—a soupcon of peculiarity which is entirely lacking to fashionable London. Then, it must be remembered that the "children of the desert" have been led by gentle degrees to understand that for harboring the strange locusts imported into their land by Cook, and the still stranger specimens of unclassified insect called Upper Ten, which imports itself, they will receive "backsheesh."

"Backsheesh" is a certain source of comfort to all nations, and translates itself with sweetest euphony into all languages, and the desert-born tribes have justice on their side when they demand as much of it as they can get, rightfully or wrongfully. They deserve to gain some sort of advantage out of the odd-looking swarms of Western invaders who amaze them by their dress and affront them by their manners. "Backsheesh," therefore, has become the perpetual cry of the Desert-Born,—it is the only means of offence and defence left to them, and very naturally they cling to it with fervor and resolution. And who shall blame them? The tall, majestic, meditative Arab—superb as mere man, and standing naked-footed on his sandy native soil, with his one rough garment flung round his loins and his great black eyes fronting, eagle-like, the sun—merits something considerable for condescending to act as guide and servant to the Western moneyed civilian who clothes his lower limbs in straight, funnel-like cloth casings, shaped to the strict resemblance of an elephant's legs, and finishes the graceful design by enclosing the rest of his body in a stiff shirt wherein he can scarcely move, and a square-cut coat which divides him neatly in twain by a line immediately above the knee, with the effect of lessening his height by several inches. The Desert-Born surveys him gravely and in civil compassion, sometimes with a muttered prayer against the hideousness of him, but on the whole with patience and equanimity,—influenced by considerations of "backsheesh." And the English "season" whirls lightly and vaporously, like blown egg-froth, over the mystic land of the old gods,—the terrible land filled with dark secrets as yet unexplored,—the land "shadowing with wings," as the Bible hath it,—the land in which are buried tremendous histories as yet unguessed,—profound enigmas of the supernatural,—labyrinths of wonder, terror and mystery,—all of which remain unrevealed to the giddy-pated, dancing, dining, gabbling throng of the fashionable travelling lunatics of the day,—the people who "never think because it is too much trouble," people whose one idea is to journey from hotel to hotel and compare notes with their acquaintances afterwards as to which house provided them with the best-cooked food. For it is a noticeable fact that with most visitors to the "show" places of Europe and the East, food, bedding and selfish personal comfort are the first considerations,—the scenery and the associations come last. Formerly the position was reversed. In the days when there were no railways, and the immortal Byron wrote his Childe Harold, it was customary to rate personal inconvenience lightly; the beautiful or historic scene was the attraction for the traveller, and not the arrangements made for his special form of digestive apparatus. Byron could sleep on the deck of a sailing vessel wrapped in his cloak and feel none the worse for it; his well-braced mind and aspiring spirit soared above all bodily discomforts; his thoughts were engrossed with the mighty teachings of time; he was able to lose himself in glorious reveries on the lessons of the past and the possibilities of the future; the attitude of the inspired Thinker as well as Poet was his, and a crust of bread and cheese served him as sufficiently on his journeyings among the then unspoilt valleys and mountains of Switzerland as the warm, greasy, indigestible fare of the elaborate table-d'hotes at Lucerne and Interlaken serve us now. But we, in our "superior" condition, pooh-pooh the Byronic spirit of indifference to events and scorn of trifles,—we say it is "melodramatic," completely forgetting that our attitude towards ourselves and things in general is one of most pitiable bathos. We cannot write Childe Harold, but we can grumble at both bed and board in every hotel under the sun; we can discover teasing midges in the air and questionable insects in the rooms; and we can discuss each bill presented to us with an industrious persistence which nearly drives landlords frantic and ourselves as well. In these kind of important matters we are indeed "superior" to Byron and other ranting dreamers of his type, but we produce no Childe Harolds, and we have come to the strange pass of pretending that Don Juan is improper, while we pore over Zola with avidity! To such a pitch has our culture brought us! And, like the Pharisee in the Testament, we thank God we are not as others are. We are glad we are not as the Arab, as the African, as the Hindoo; we are proud of our elephant-legs and our dividing coat-line; these things show we are civilized, and that God approves of us more than any other type of creature ever created. We take possession of nations, not by thunder of war, but by clatter of dinner-plates. We do not raise armies, we build hotels; and we settle ourselves in Egypt as we do at Homburg, to dress and dine and sleep and sniff contempt on all things but ourselves, to such an extent that we have actually got into the habit of calling the natives of the places we usurp "foreigners." WE are the foreigners; but somehow we never can see it. Wherever we condescend to build hotels, that spot we consider ours. We are surprised at the impertinence of Frankfort people who presume to visit Homburg while we are having our "season" there; we wonder how they dare do it! And, of a truth, they seem amazed at their own boldness, and creep shyly through the Kur-Garten as though fearing to be turned out by the custodians. The same thing occurs in Egypt; we are frequently astounded at what we call "the impertinence of these foreigners," i.e. the natives. They ought to be proud to have us and our elephant-legs; glad to see such noble and beautiful types of civilization as the stout parvenu with his pendant paunch, and his family of gawky youths and maidens of the large-toothed, long-limbed genus; glad to see the English "mamma," who never grows old, but wears young hair in innocent curls, and has her wrinkles annually "massaged" out by a Paris artiste in complexion. The Desert-Born, we say, should be happy and grateful to see such sights, and not demand so much "backsheesh." In fact, the Desert-Born should not get so much in our way as he does; he is a very good servant, of course, but as a man and a brother—pooh! Egypt may be his country, and he may love it as much as we love England; but our feelings are more to be considered than his, and there is no connecting link of human sympathy between Elephant-Legs and sun-browned Nudity!

So at least thought Sir Chetwynd Lyle, a stout gentleman of coarse build and coarser physiognomy, as he sat in a deep arm-chair in the great hall or lounge of the Gezireh Palace Hotel, smoking after dinner in the company of two or three acquaintances with whom he had fraternized during his stay in Cairo. Sir Chetwynd was fond of airing his opinions for the benefit of as many people who cared to listen to him, and Sir Chetwynd had some right to his opinions, inasmuch as he was the editor and proprietor of a large London newspaper. His knighthood was quite a recent distinction, and nobody knew exactly how he had managed to get it. He had originally been known in Fleet Street by the irreverent sobriquet of "greasy Chetwynd," owing to his largeness, oiliness and general air of blandly-meaningless benevolence. He had a wife and two daughters, and one of his objects in wintering at Cairo was to get his cherished children married. It was time, for the bloom was slightly off the fair girl-roses,—the dainty petals of the delicate buds were beginning to wither. And Sir Chetwynd had heard much of Cairo; he understood that there was a great deal of liberty allowed there between men and maids,—that they went out together on driving excursions to the Pyramids, that they rode on lilliputian donkeys over the sand at moonlight, that they floated about in boats at evening on the Nile, and that, in short, there were more opportunities of marriage among the "flesh-pots of Egypt" than in all the rush and crush of London. So here he was, portly and comfortable, and on the whole well satisfied with his expedition; there were a good many eligible bachelors about, and Muriel and Dolly were really doing their best. So was their mother, Lady Chetwynd Lyle; she allowed no "eligible" to escape her hawk-like observation, and on this particular evening she was in all her glory, for there was to be a costume ball at the Gezireh Palace Hotel,—a superb affair, organized by the proprietors for the amusement of their paying guests, who certainly paid well,—even stiffly. Owing to the preparations that were going on for this festivity, the lounge, with its sumptuous Egyptian decorations and luxurious modern fittings, was well-nigh deserted save for Sir Chetwynd and his particular group of friends, to whom he was holding forth, between slow cigar-puffs, on the squalor of the Arabs, the frightful thievery of the Sheiks, the incompetency of his own special dragoman, and the mistake people made in thinking the Egyptians themselves a fine race.

"They are tall, certainly," said Sir Chetwynd, surveying his paunch, which lolled comfortably, and as it were by itself, in front of him, like a kind of waistcoated air-balloon. "I grant you they are tall. That is, the majority of them are. But I have seen short men among them. The Khedive is not taller than I am. And the Egyptian face is very deceptive. The features are often fine,—occasionally classic,—but intelligent expression is totally lacking."

Here Sir Chetwynd waved his cigar descriptively, as though he would fain suggest that a heavy jaw, a fat nose with a pimple at the end, and a gross mouth with black teeth inside it, which were special points in his own physiognomy, went further to make up "intelligent expression" than any well-moulded, straight, Eastern type of sun-browned countenance ever seen or imagined.

"Well, I don't quite agree with you there," said a man who was lying full length on one of the divans close by and smoking. "These brown chaps have deuced fine eyes. There doesn't seem to be any lack of expression in them. And that reminds me, there is at fellow arrived here to-day who looks for all the world like an Egyptian, of the best form. He is a Frenchman, though; a Provencal,—every one knows him,—he is the famous painter, Armand Gervase."

"Indeed!"—and Sir Chetwynd roused himself at the name—"Armand Gervase! THE Armand Gervase?"

"The only one original," laughed the other. "He's come here to make studies of Eastern women. A rare old time he'll have among them, I daresay! He's not famous for character. He ought to paint the Princess Ziska."

"Ah, by-the-bye, I wanted to ask you about that lady. Does anyone know who she is? My wife is very anxious to find out whether she is— well—er—quite the proper person, you know! When one has young girls, one cannot be too careful."

Ross Courtney, the man on the divan, got up slowly and stretched his long athletic limbs with a lazy enjoyment in the action. He was a sporting person with unhampered means and large estates in Scotland and Ireland; he lived a joyous, "don't-care" life of wandering about the world in search of adventures, and he had a scorn of civilized conventionalities—newspapers and their editors among them. And whenever Sir Chetwynd spoke of his "young girls" he was moved to irreverent smiling, as he knew the youngest of the twain was at least thirty. He also recognized and avoided the wily traps and pitfalls set for him by Lady Chetwynd Lyle in the hope that he would yield himself up a captive to the charms of Muriel or Dolly; and as he thought of these two fair ones now and involuntarily compared them in his mind with the other woman just spoken of, the smile that had begun to hover on his lips deepened unconsciously till his handsome face was quite illumined with its mirth.

"Upon my word, I don't think it matters who anybody is in Cairo!" he said with a fine carelessness. "The people whose families are all guaranteed respectable are more lax in their behavior than the people one knows nothing about. As for the Princess Ziska, her extraordinary beauty and intelligence would give her the entree anywhere—even if she hadn't money to back those qualities up."

"She's enormously wealthy, I hear," said young Lord Fulkeward, another of the languid smokers, caressing his scarcely perceptible moustache. "My mother thinks she is a divorcee."

Sir Chetwynd looked very serious, and shook his fat head solemnly.

"Well, there is nothing remarkable in being divorced, you know," laughed Ross Courtney. "Nowadays it seems the natural and fitting end of marriage."

Sir Chetwynd looked graver still. He refused to be drawn into this kind of flippant conversation. He, at any rate, was respectably married; he had no sympathy whatever with the larger majority of people whose marriages were a failure.

"There is no Prince Ziska then?" he inquired. "The name sounds to me of Russian origin, and I imagined—my wife also imagined,—that the husband of the lady might very easily be in Russia while his wife's health might necessitate her wintering in Egypt. The Russian winter climate is inclement, I believe."

"That would be a very neat arrangement," yawned Lord Fulkeward. "But my mother thinks not. My mother thinks there is not a husband at all,—that there never was a husband. In fact my mother has very strong convictions on the subject. But my mother intends to visit her all the same."

"She does? Lady Fulkeward has decided on that? Oh, well, in THAT case!"—and Sir Chetwynd expanded his lower-chest air-balloon. "Of course, Lady Chetwynd Lyle can no longer have any scruples on the subject. If Lady Fulkeward visits the Princess there can be no doubt as to her actual STATUS."

"Oh, I don't know!" murmured Lord Fulkeward, stroking his downy lip. "You see my mother's rather an exceptional person. When the governor was alive she hardly ever went out anywhere, you know, and all the people who came to our house in Yorkshire had to bring their pedigrees with them, so to speak. It was beastly dull! But now my mother has taken to 'studying character,' don'cher know; she likes all sorts of people about her, and the more mixed they are the more she is delighted with them. Fact, I assure you! Quite a change has come over my mother since the poor old governor died!"

Ross Courtney looked amused. A change indeed had come over Lady Fulkeward—a change, sudden, mysterious and amazing to many of her former distinguished friends with "pedigrees." In her husband's lifetime her hair had been a soft silver-gray; her face pale, refined and serious; her form full and matronly; her step sober and discreet; but two years after the death of the kindly and noble old lord who had cherished her as the apple of his eye and up to the last moment of his breath had thought her the most beautiful woman in England, she appeared with golden tresses, a peach-bloom complexion, and a figure which had been so massaged, rubbed, pressed and artistically corseted as to appear positively sylph-like. She danced like a fairy, she who had once been called "old" Lady Fulkeward; she smoked cigarettes; she laughed like a child at every trivial thing—any joke, however stale, flat and unprofitable, was sufficient to stir her light pulses to merriment; and she flirted—oh, heavens!—How she flirted!—with a skill and a grace and a knowledge and an aplomb that nearly drove Muriel and Dolly Chetwynd Lyle frantic. They, poor things, were beaten out of the field altogether by her superior tact and art of "fence," and they hated her accordingly and called her in private a "horrid old woman," which perhaps, when her maid undressed her, she was. But she was having a distinctly "good time" in Cairo; she called her son, who was in delicate health, "my poor dear little boy!" and he, though twenty-eight on his last birthday, was reduced to such an abject condition of servitude by her assertiveness, impudent gayety and general freedom of manner, that he could not open his mouth without alluding to "my mother," and using "my mother" as a peg whereon to hang all his own opinions and emotions as well as the opinions and emotions of other people.

"Lady Fulkeward admires the Princess very much, I believe?" said another lounger who had not yet spoken.

"Oh, as to that!"—and Lord Fulkeward roused himself to some faint show of energy. "Who wouldn't admire her? By Jove! Only, I tell you what—there's something I weird about her eyes. Fact! I don't like her eyes."

"Shut up, Fulke! She has beautiful eyes!" burst out Courtney, hotly; then flushing suddenly he bit his lips and was silent.

"Who is this that has beautiful eyes?" suddenly demanded a slow, gruff voice, and a little thin gentleman, dressed in a kind of academic gown and cap, appeared on the scene.

"Hullo! here's our F.R.S.A.!" exclaimed Lord Fulkeward. "By Jove! Is that the style you have got yourself up in for tonight? It looks awfully smart, don'cher know!"

The personage thus complimented adjusted his spectacles and surveyed his acquaintances with a very well-satisfied air. In truth, Dr. Maxwell Dean had some reason for self-satisfaction, if the knowledge that he possessed one of the cleverest heads in Europe could give a man cause for pride. He was apparently the only individual in the Gezireh Palace Hotel who had come to Egypt for any serious purpose. A purpose he had, though what it was he declined to explain. Reticent, often brusque, and sometimes mysterious in his manner of speech, there was not the slightest doubt that he was at work on something, and that he also had a very trying habit of closely studying every object, small or great, that came under his observation. He studied the natives to such an extent that he knew every differing shade of color in their skins; he studied Sir Chetwynd Lyle and knew that he occasionally took bribes to "put things" into his paper; he studied Dolly and Muriel Chetwynd Lyle, and knew that they would never succeed in getting husbands; he studied Lady Fulkeward, and thought her very well got up for sixty; he studied Ross Courtney, and knew he would never do anything but kill animals all his life; and he studied the working of the Gezireh Palace Hotel, and saw a fortune rising out of it for the proprietors. But apart from these ordinary surface things, he studied other matters—"occult" peculiarities of temperament, "coincidences," strange occurrences generally. He could read the Egyptian hieroglyphs perfectly, and he understood the difference between "royal cartouche" scarabei and Birmingham-manufactured ones. He was never dull; he had plenty to do; and he took everything as it came in its turn. Even the costume ball for which he had now attired himself did not present itself to him as a "bore," but as a new vein of information, opening to him fresh glimpses of the genus homo as seen in a state of eccentricity.

"I think," he now said, complacently, "that the cap and gown look well for a man of my years. It is a simple garb, but cool, convenient and not unbecoming. I had thought at first of adopting the dress of an ancient Egyptian priest, but I find it difficult to secure the complete outfit. I would never wear a costume of the kind that was not in every point historically correct."

No one smiled. No one would have dared to smile at Dr. Maxwell

Dean when he spoke of "historically correct" things. He had studied them as he had studied everything, and he knew all about them.

Sir Chetwynd murmured:

"Quite right—er—the ancient designs were very elaborate—"

"And symbolic," finished Dr. Dean. "Symbolic of very curious meanings, I assure you. But I fear I have interrupted your talk. Mr. Courtney was speaking about somebody's beautiful eyes; who is the fair one in question?"

"The Princess Ziska," said Lord Fulkeward. "I was saying that I don't quite like the look of her eyes."

"Why not? Why not?" demanded the doctor with sudden asperity. "What's the matter with them?"

"Everything's the matter with them!" replied Ross Courtney with a forced laugh. "They are too splendid and wild for Fulke; he likes the English pale-blue better than the Egyptian gazelle-black."

"No, I don't," said Lord Fulkeward, speaking more animatedly than was customary with him. "I hate, pale-blue eyes. I prefer soft violet-gray ones, like Miss Murray's."

"Miss Helen Murray is a very charming young lady," said Dr. Dean. "But her beauty is quite an ordinary type, while that of the Princess Ziska—"

"Is EXTRA-ordinary—exactly! That's just what I say!" declared Courtney. "I think she is the loveliest woman I have ever seen."

There was a pause, during which the little doctor looked with a ferret-like curiosity from one man to the other. Sir Chetwynd Lyle rose ponderously up from the depths of his arm-chair.

"I think," said he, "I had better go and get into my uniform—the Windsor, you know! I always have it with me wherever I go; it comes in very useful for fancy balls such as the one we are going to have tonight, when no particular period is observed in costume. Isn't it about time we all got ready?"

"Upon my life, I think it is!" agreed Lord Fulkeward. "I am coming out as a Neapolitan fisherman! I don't believe Neapolitan fishermen ever really dress in the way I'm going to make up, but it's the accepted stage-type, don'cher know."

"Ah! I daresay you will look very well in it," murmured Ross Courtney, vaguely. "Hullo! here comes Denzil Murray!"

They all turned instinctively to watch the entrance of a handsome young man, attired in the picturesque garb worn by Florentine nobles during the prosperous reign of the Medicis. It was a costume admirably adapted to the wearer, who, being grave and almost stern of feature, needed the brightness of jewels and the gloss of velvet and satin to throw out the classic contour of his fine head and enhance the lustre of his brooding, darkly-passionate eyes. Denzil Murray was a pure-blooded Highlander,—the level brows, the firm lips, the straight, fearless look, all bespoke him a son of the heather-crowned mountains and a descendant of the proud races that scorned the "Sassenach," and retained sufficient of the material whereof their early Phoenician ancestors were made to be capable of both the extremes of hate and love in their most potent forms. He moved slowly towards the group of men awaiting his approach with a reserved air of something like hauteur; it was possible he was conscious of his good looks, but it was equally evident that he did not desire to be made the object of impertinent remark. His friends silently recognized this, and only Lord Fulkeward, moved to a mild transport of admiration, ventured to comment on his appearance.

"I say, Denzil, you're awfully well got up! Awfully well! Magnificent!"

Denzil Murray bowed with a somewhat wearied and sarcastic air.

"When one is in Rome, or Egypt, one must do as Rome, or Egypt, does," he said, carelessly. "If hotel proprietors will give fancy balls, it is necessary to rise to the occasion. You look very well, Doctor. Why don't you other fellows go and get your toggeries on? It's past ten o'clock, and the Princess Ziska will be here by eleven."

"There are other people coming besides the Princess Ziska, are there not, Mr. Murray?" inquired Sir Chetwynd Lyle, with an obtrusively bantering air.

Denzil Murray glanced him over disdainfully.

"I believe there are," he answered coolly. "Otherwise the ball would scarcely pay its expenses. But as the Princess is admittedly the most beautiful woman in Cairo this season, she will naturally be the centre of attraction. That's why I mentioned she would be here at eleven."

"She told you that?" inquired Ross Courtney.

"She did."

Courtney looked up, then down, and seemed about to speak again, but checked himself and finally strolled off, followed by Lord Fulkeward.

"I hear," said Dr. Dean then, addressing Denzil Murray, "that a great celebrity has arrived at this hotel—the painter, Armand Gervase."

Denzil's face brightened instantly with a pleasant smile.

"The dearest friend I have in the world!" he said. "Yes, he is here. I met him outside the door this afternoon. We are very old chums. I have stayed with him in Paris, and he has stayed with me in Scotland. A charming fellow! He is very French in his ideas; but he knows England well, and speaks English perfectly."

"French in his ideas!" echoed Sir Chetwynd Lyle, who was just preparing to leave the lounge. "Dear me! How is that?"

"He is a Frenchman," said Dr. Dean, suavely. "Therefore that his ideas should be French ought not to be a matter of surprise to us, my dear Sir Chetwynd."

Sir Chetwynd snorted. He had a suspicion that he—the editor and proprietor of the Daily Dial—was being laughed at, and he at once clambered on his high horse of British Morality.

"Frenchman or no Frenchman," he observed, "the ideas promulgated in France at the present day are distinctly profane and pernicious. There is a lack of principle—a want of rectitude in—er—the French Press, for example, that is highly deplorable."

"And is the English Press immaculate?" asked Denzil languidly.

"We hope so," replied Sir Chetwynd. "We do our best to make it so."

And with that remark he took his paunch and himself away into retirement, leaving Dr. Dean and young Murray facing each other, a singular pair enough in the contrast of their appearance and dress,—the one small, lean and wiry, in plain-cut, loose-flowing academic gown; the other tall, broad and muscular, clad in the rich attire of mediaeval Florence, and looking for all the world like a fine picture of that period stepped out from, its frame. There was a silence between them for a moment,—then the Doctor spoke in a low tone:

"It won't do, my dear boy,—I assure you it won't do! You will break your heart over a dream, and make yourself miserable for nothing. And you will break your sister's heart as well; perhaps you haven't thought of that?"

Denzil flung himself into the chair Sir Chetwynd had just vacated, and gave vent to a sigh that was almost a groan.

"Helen doesn't know anything—yet," he said hoarsely. "I know nothing myself; how can I? I haven't said a word to—to HER. If I spoke all that was in my mind, I daresay she would laugh at me. You are the only one who has guessed my secret. You saw me last night when I— when I accompanied her home. But I never passed her palace gates,— she wouldn't let me. She bade me 'good-night' outside; a servant admitted her, and she vanished through the portal like a witch or a ghost. Sometimes I fancy she Is a ghost. She is so white, so light, so noiseless and so lovely!"

He turned his eyes away, ashamed of the emotion that moved him. Dr. Maxwell Dean took off his academic cap and examined its interior as though he considered it remarkable.

"Yes," he said slowly; "I have thought the same thing of her myself—sometimes."

Further conversation was interrupted by the entrance of the military band of the evening, which now crossed the "lounge," each man carrying his instrument with him; and these were followed by several groups of people in fancy dress, all ready and eager for the ball. Pierrots and Pierrettes, monks in drooping cowls, flower-girls, water-carriers, symbolic figures of "Night" and "Morning," mingled with the counterfeit presentments of dead-and-gone kings and queens, began to flock together, laughing and talking on their way to the ball-room; and presently among them came a man whose superior height and build, combined with his eminently picturesque, half-savage type of beauty, caused every one to turn and watch him as he passed, and murmur whispering comments on the various qualities wherein he differed from themselves. He was attired for the occasion as a Bedouin chief, and his fierce black eyes, and close-curling, dark hair, combined with the natural olive tint of his complexion, were well set off by the snowy folds of his turban and the whiteness of his entire costume, which was unrelieved by any color save at the waist, where a gleam of scarlet was shown in the sash which helped to fasten a murderous-looking dagger and other "correct" weapons of attack to his belt. He entered the hall with a swift and singularly light step, and made straight for Denzil Murray.

"Ah! here you are!" he said, speaking English with a slight foreign accent, which was more agreeable to the ear than otherwise. "But, my excellent boy, what magnificence! A Medici costume! Never say to me that you are not vain; you are as conscious of your good looks as any pretty woman. Behold me, how simple and unobtrusive I am!"

He laughed, and Murray sprang up from the chair where he had been despondently reclining.

"Oh, come, I like that!" he exclaimed. "Simple and unobtrusive! Why everybody is staring at you now as if you had dropped from the moon! You cannot be Armand Gervase and simple and unobtrusive at the same time!"

"Why not?" demanded Gervase, lightly. "Fame is capricious, and her trumpet is not loud enough to be heard all over the world at once. The venerable proprietor of the dirty bazaar where I managed to purchase these charming articles of Bedouin costume had never heard of me in his life. Miserable man! He does not know what he has missed!"

Here his flashing black eyes lit suddenly on Dr. Dean, who was "studying" him in the same sort of pertinacious way in which that learned little man studied everything.

"A friend of yours, Denzil?" he inquired.

"Yes," responded Murray readily; "a very great friend—Dr. Maxwell Dean. Dr. Dean, let me introduce to you Armand Gervase; I need not explain him further!"

"You need not, indeed!" said the doctor, with a ceremonious bow. "The name is one of universal celebrity."

"It is not always an advantage—this universal celebrity," replied Gervase. "Nor is it true that any celebrity is actually universal. Perhaps the only living person that is universally known, by name at least, is Zola. Mankind are at one in their appreciation of vice."

"I cannot altogether agree with you there," said Dr. Dean slowly, keeping his gaze fixed on the artist's bold, proud features with singular curiosity. "The French Academy, I presume, are individually as appreciative of human weaknesses as most men; but taken collectively, some spirit higher and stronger than their own keeps them unanimous in their rejection of the notorious Realist who sacrifices all the canons of art and beauty to the discussion of topics unmentionable in decent society."

Gervase laughed idly.

"Oh, he will get in some day, you may be sure," he answered. "There is no spirit higher and stronger than the spirit of naturalism in man; and in time, when a few prejudices have died away and mawkish sentiment has been worn threadbare, Zola will be enrolled as the first of the French Academicians, with even more honors than if he had succeeded in the beginning. That is the way of all those 'select' bodies. As Napoleon said, 'Le monde vient a celui qui sait attendre.'"

The little Doctor's countenance now showed the most lively and eager interest.

"You quite believe that, Monsieur Gervase? You are entirely sure of what you said just now?"

"What did I say? I forget!" smiled Gervase, lighting a cigarette and beginning to smoke it leisurely.

"You said, 'There is no spirit higher or stronger than the spirit of naturalism in man.' Are you positive on this point?"

"Why, of course! Most entirely positive!" And the great painter looked amused as he gave the reply. "Naturalism is Nature, or the things appertaining to Nature, and there is nothing higher or stronger than Nature everywhere and anywhere."

"How about God?" inquired Dr. Dean with a curious air, as if he were propounding a remarkable conundrum.

"God!" Gervase laughed loudly. "Pardon! Are you a clergyman?"

"By no means!" and the Doctor gave a little bow and deprecating smile. "I am not in any way connected with the Church. I am a doctor of laws and literature,—a humble student of philosophy and science generally. . ."

"Philosophy! Science!" interrupted Gervase. "And you ask about God! Parbleu! Science and philosophy have progressed beyond Him!"

"Exactly!" and Dr. Dean rubbed his hands together pleasantly. "That is your opinion? Yes, I thought so! Science and philosophy, to put it comprehensively, have beaten poor God on His own ground! Ha! ha! ha! Very good—very good! And humorous as well! Ha! ha!"

And a very droll appearance just then had this "humble student of philosophy and science generally," for he bent himself to and fro with laughter, and his small eyes almost disappeared behind his shelving brows in the excess of his mirth. And two crosslines formed themselves near his thin mouth—such lines as are carven on the ancient Greek masks which indicate satire.

Denzil Murray flushed uncomfortably.

"Gervase doesn't believe in anything but Art," he said, as though half apologizing for his friend: "Art is the sole object of his existence; I don't believe he ever has time to think about anything else."

"Of what else should I think, mon ami?" exclaimed Gervase mirthfully. "Of life? It is all Art to me; and by Art I mean the idealization and transfiguration of Nature."

"Oh. if you do that sort of thing you are a romancist," interposed Dr. Dean emphatically. "Nature neither idealizes nor transfigures itself; it is simply Nature and no more. Matter uncontrolled by Spirit is anything but ideal."

"Precisely," answered Gervase quickly and with some warmth; "but my spirit idealizes it,—my imagination sees beyond it,—my soul grasps it."

"Oh, you have a soul?" exclaimed Dr. Dean, beginning to laugh again. "Now, how did you find that out?"

Gervase looked at him in a sudden surprise.

"Every man has an inward self, naturally," he said. "We call it 'soul' as a figure of speech; it is really temperament merely."

"Oh, it is merely temperament? Then you don't think it is likely to outlive you, this soul—to take new phases upon itself and go on existing, an immortal being, when your body is in a far worse condition (because less carefully preserved) than an Egyptian mummy?"

"Certainly not!" and Gervase flung away the end of his finished cigarette. "The immortality of the soul is quite an exploded theory. It was always a ridiculous one. We have quite enough to vex us in our present life, and why men ever set about inventing another is more than I am able to understand. It was a most foolish and barbaric superstition."

The gay sound of music now floated towards them from the ball-room,—the strains of a graceful, joyous, half-commanding, half-pleading waltz came rhythmically beating on the air like the measured movement of wings,—and Denzil Murray, beginning to grow restless, walked to and fro, his eyes watching every figure that crossed and re-crossed the hall. But Dr. Dean's interest in Armand Gervase remained intense and unabated; and approaching him, he laid two lean fingers delicately on the white folds of the Bedouin dress just where the heart of the man was hidden.

"'A foolish and barbaric superstition!'" he echoed slowly and meditatively. "You do not believe in any possibility of there being a life—or several lives—after this present death through which we must all pass inevitably, sooner or later?"

"Not in the least! I leave such ideas to the ignorant and uneducated. I should be unworthy of the progressive teachings of my time if I believed such arrant nonsense."

"Death, you consider, finishes all? There is nothing further—no mysteries beyond? . . ." and Dr. Dean's eyes glittered as he stretched forth one thin, slight hand and pointed into space with the word "beyond," an action which gave it a curious emphasis, and for a fleeting second left a weird impression on even the careless mind of Gervase. But he laughed it off lightly.

"Nothing beyond? Of course not! My dear sir, why ask such a question? Nothing can be plainer or more positive than the fact that death, as you say, finishes all."

A woman's laugh, low and exquisitely musical, rippled on the air as he spoke—delicious laughter, rarer than song; for women as a rule laugh too loudly, and the sound of their merriment partakes more of the nature of a goose's cackle than any other sort of natural melody. But this large, soft and silvery, was like a delicately subdued cadence played on a magic flute in the distance, and suggested nothing but sweetness; and at the sound of it Gervase started violently and turned sharply round upon his friend Murray with a look of wonderment and perplexity.

"Who is that?" he demanded. "I have heard that pretty laugh before; it must be some one I know."

But Denzil scarcely heard him. Pale, and with eyes full of yearning and passion, he was watching the slow approach of a group of people in fancy dress, who were all eagerly pressing round one central figure— the figure of a woman clad in gleaming golden tissues and veiled in the old Egyptian fashion up to the eyes, with jewels flashing about her waist, bosom and hair,—a woman who moved glidingly as if she floated rather than walked, and whose beauty, half hidden as it was by the exigencies of the costume she had chosen, was so unusual and brilliant that it seemed to create an atmosphere of bewilderment and rapture around her as she came. She was preceded by a small Nubian boy in a costume of vivid scarlet, who, walking backwards humbly, fanned her slowly with a tall fan of peacock's plumes made after the quaint designs of ancient Egypt. The lustre radiating from the peacock's feathers, the light of her golden garments, her jewels and the marvellous black splendor of her eyes, all flashed for a moment like sudden lightning on Gervase; something—he knew not what—turned him giddy and blind; hardly knowing what he did, he sprang eagerly forward, when all at once he felt the lean, small hand of Dr. Dean on his arm and stopped short embarrassed.

"Pardon me!" said the little savant, with a delicate, half-supercilious lifting of his eyebrows. "But—do you know the Princess Ziska?"

MARIE CORELLI

II

Gervase stared at him, still dazzled and confused.

"Whom did you say? . . . the Princess Ziska? . . . No, I don't know her. . . Yet, stay! Yes, I think I have seen her. . . somewhere,—in Paris, possibly. Will you introduce me?"

"I leave that duty to Mr. Denzil Murray," said the Doctor, folding his arms neatly behind his back. . . "He knows her better than I do."

And smiling his little grim, cynical smile, he settled his academic cap more firmly on his head and strolled off towards the ballroom. Gervase stood irresolute, his eyes fixed on that wondrous golden figure that floated before his eyes like an aerial vision. Denzil Murray had gone forward to meet the Princess and was now talking to her, his handsome face radiating with the admiration he made no attempt to conceal. After a little pause Gervase moved towards him a step or two, and caught part of the conversation.

"You look the very beau-ideal of an Egyptian Princess," Murray was saying. "Your costume is perfect."

She laughed. Again that sweet, rare laughter! Gervase thrilled with the pulsation of it,—it beat in his ears and smote his brain with a strange echo of familiarity.

"Is it not?" she responded. "I am 'historically correct,' as your friend Dr. Dean would say. My ornaments are genuine,—they all came out of the same tomb."

"I find one fault with your attire, Princess," said one of the male admirers who had entered with her; "part of your face is veiled. That is a cruelty to us all!"

She waived the compliment aside with a light gesture.

"It was the fashion in ancient Egypt," she said. "Love in those old days was not what it is now,—one glance, one smile was sufficient to set the soul on fire and draw another soul towards it to consume together in the suddenly kindled flame! And women veiled their faces in youth, lest they should be deemed too prodigal of their charms; and in age they covered themselves still more closely, in order not to affront the Sun-God's fairness by their wrinkles." She smiled, a dazzling smile that drew Gervase yet a few steps closer unconsciously, as though he were being magnetized. "But I am not bound to keep the veil always up," and as she spoke she loosened it and let it fall, showing an exquisite face, fair as a lily, and of such perfect loveliness that the men who were gathered round her seemed to lose breath and speech at sight of it. "That pleases you better, Mr. Murray?"

Denzil grew very pale. Bending down he murmured something to her in a low tone. She raised her lovely brows with a little touch of surprise that was half disdain, and looked at him straightly.

"You say very pretty things; but they do not always please me," she observed. "However, that is my fault, no doubt."

And she began to move onwards, her Nubian page preceding her as before. Gervase stood in her path and confronted her as she came.

"Introduce me," he said in a commanding tone to Denzil.

Denzil looked at him, somewhat startled by the suppressed passion in his voice.

"Certainly. Princess, permit me!" She paused, a figure of silent grace and attention. "Allow me to present to you my friend, Armand Gervase, the most famous artist in France—Gervase, the Princess Ziska."

She raised her deep, dark eyes and fixed them on his face, and as he looked boldly at her in a kind of audacious admiration, he felt again that strange dizzying shock which had before thrilled him through and through. There was something strangely familiar about her; the faint odors that seemed exhaled from her garments,—the gleam of the jewel-winged scarabei on her breast,—the weird light of the emerald-studded serpent in her hair; and more, much more familiar than these trifles, was the sound of her voice—dulcet, penetrating, grave and haunting in its tone.

"At last we meet, Monsieur Armand Gervase!" she said slowly and with a graceful inclination of her head. "But I cannot look upon you as a stranger, for I have known you so long—in spirit!"

She smiled—a strange smile, dazzling yet enigmatical—and something wild and voluptuous seemed to stir in Gervase's pulses as he touched the small hand, loaded with quaint Egyptian gems, which she graciously extended towards him.

"I think I have known you, too!" he said. "Possibly in a dream,—a dream of beauty never realized till now!"

His voice sank to an amorous whisper; but she said nothing in reply, nor could her looks be construed into any expression of either pleasure or offence. Yet through the heart of young Denzil Murray went a sudden pang of jealousy, and for the first time in his life he became conscious that even among men as well as women there may exist what is called the "petty envy" of a possible rival, and the uneasy desire to outshine such an one in all points of appearance, dress and manner. His gaze rested broodingly on the tall, muscular form of Gervase, and he noted the symmetry and supple grace of the man with an irritation of which he was ashamed. He knew, despite his own undeniably handsome personality, which was set off to such advantage that night by the richness of the Florentine costume he had adopted, that there was a certain fascination about Gervase which was inborn, a trick of manner which made him seem picturesque at all times; and that even when the great French artist had stayed with him in Scotland and got himself up for the occasion in more or less baggy tweeds, people were fond of remarking that the only man who ever succeeded in making tweeds look artistic was Armand Gervase. And in the white Bedouin garb he now wore he was seen at his best; a certain restless passion betrayed in eyes and lips made him look the savage part he had "dressed" for, and as he bent his head over the Princess Ziska's hand and kissed it with an odd mingling of flippancy and reverence, Denzil suddenly began to think how curiously alike they were, these two! Strong man and fair woman, both had many physical points in common,—the same dark, level brows,—the same half wild, half tender eyes,—the same sinuous grace of form,—the same peculiar lightness of movement,—and yet both were different, while resembling each other. It was not what is called a "family likeness" which existed between them; it was the cast of countenance or "type" that exists between races or tribes, and had young Murray not known his friend Gervase to be a French Provencal and equally understood the Princess Ziska to be of Russian origin, he would have declared them both, natives of Egypt, of the purest caste and highest breeding. He was so struck by this idea that he might have spoken his thought aloud had he not heard Gervase boldly arranging dance after dance with the Princess, and apparently preparing to write no name but hers down the entire length of his ball programme,—a piece of audacity which had the effect of rousing Denzil to assert his own rights.

"You promised me the first waltz, Princess," he said, his face flushing as he spoke.

"Quite true! And you shall have it," she replied, smiling. "Monsieur Gervase will have the second. The music sounds very inviting; shall we not go in?"

"We spoil the effect of your entree crowding about you like this," said Denzil, glancing somewhat sullenly at Gervase and the other men surrounding her; "and, by the way, you have never told us what character you represent to-night; some great queen of old time, no doubt?"

"No, I lay no claim to sovereignty," she answered; "I am for to-night the living picture of a once famous and very improper person who bore half my name, a dancer of old time, known as 'Ziska-Charmazel,' the favorite of the harem of a great Egyptian warrior, described in forgotten histories as 'The Mighty Araxes.'"

She paused; her admirers, fascinated by the sound of her voice, were all silent. She fixed her eyes upon Gervase; and addressing him only, continued:

"Yes, I am 'Charmazel,'" she said. "She was, as I tell you, an 'improper' person, or would be so considered by the good English people. Because, you know, she was never married to Araxes!"

This explanation, given with the demurest naivete, caused a laugh among her listeners.

"That wouldn't make her 'improper' in France," said Gervase gayly. "She would only seem more interesting."

"Ah! Then modern France is like old Egypt?" she queried, still smiling. "And Frenchmen can be found perhaps who are like Araxes in the number of their loves and infidelities?"

"I should say my country is populated entirely with copies of him," replied Gervase, mirthfully. "Was he a very distinguished personage?"

"He was. Old legends say he was the greatest warrior of his time; as you, Monsieur Gervase, are the greatest artist."

Gervase bowed.

"You flatter me, fair Charmazel!" he said; then suddenly as the strange name passed his lips he recoiled as if he had been stung, and seemed for a moment dazed. The Princess turned her dark eyes on him inquiringly.

"Something troubles you, Monsieur Gervase?" she asked.

His brows knitted in a perplexed frown.

"Nothing. . . the heat. . . the air. . . a trifle, I assure you? Will you not join the dancers? Denzil, the music calls you. When your waltz with the Princess is ended I shall claim my turn. For the moment. . . au revoir!"

He stood aside and let the little group pass him by: the Princess Ziska moving with her floating, noiseless grace, Denzil Murray beside her, the little Nubian boy waving the peacock-plumes in front of them both, and all the other enslaved admirers of this singularly attractive woman crowding together behind. He watched the little cortege with strained, dim sight, till just at the dividing portal between the lounge and the ballroom the Princess turned and looked back at him with a smile. Over all the intervening heads their eyes met in one flash of mutual comprehension! then, as the fair face vanished like a light absorbed into the lights beyond it, Gervase, left alone, dropped heavily into a chair and stared vaguely at the elaborate pattern of the thick carpet at his feet. Passing his hand across his forehead he withdrew it, wet with drops of perspiration.

"What is wrong with me?" he muttered. "Am I sickening for a fever before I have been forty-eight hours in Cairo? What fool's notion is this in my brain? Where have I seen her before? In Paris? St. Petersburg? London? Charmazel! . . . Charmazel! . . . What has the name to do with me? Ziska-Charmazel! It is like the name of a romance or a gypsy tune. Bah! I must be dreaming! Her face, her eyes, are perfectly familiar; where, where have I seen her and played the mad fool with her before? Was she a model at one of the studios? Have I seen her by chance thus in her days of poverty, and does her image recall itself vividly now despite her changed surroundings? I know the very perfume of her hair. . . it seems to creep into my blood. . . it intoxicates me. . . it chokes me! . . ."

He sprang up with a fierce gesture, then after a minute's pause sat down again, and again stared at the floor.

The gay music from the ball-room danced towards him on the air in sweet, broken echoes,—he heard nothing and saw nothing.

"My God!" he said at last, under his breath. "Can it be possible that I love this woman?"

III

W ithin the ball-room the tide of gayety was rising to its height. It may be a very trivial matter, yet it is certain that fancy dress gives a peculiar charm, freedom, and brightness to festivities of the kind; and men who in the ordinary mournful black evening-suit would be taciturn of speech and conventional in bearing, throw off their customary reserve when they find themselves in the brilliant and becoming attire of some picturesque period when dress was an art as well as a fashion; and not only do they look their best, but they somehow manage to put on "manner" with costume, and to become courteous, witty, and graceful to a degree that sometimes causes their own relatives to wonder at them and speculate as to why they have grown so suddenly interesting. Few have read Sartor Resartus with either comprehension or profit, and are therefore unaware, as Teufelsdrockh was, that "Society is founded upon Cloth"—i.e. that man does adapt his manners very much to suit his clothes; and that as the costume of the days of Louis Quinze or Louis Seize inspired graceful deportment and studied courtesy to women, so does the costume of our nineteenth century inspire brusque demeanor and curt forms of speech, which, however sincere, are not flattering to the fair sex.

More love-making goes on at a fancy-dress ball than at an ordinary one; and numerous were the couples that strolled through the corridors and along the terraces of the Gezireh Palace Hotel when, after the first dozen dances were ended, it was discovered that one of the most glorious of full moons had risen over the turrets and minarets of Cairo, illumining every visible object with as clear a lustre as that of day. Then it was that warriors and nobles of mediaeval days were seen strolling with mythological goddesses and out-of-date peasants of Italy and Spain; then audacious "toreadors" were perceived whispering in the ears of crowned queens, and clowns were caught lingering amorously by the side of impossible flower-girls of all nations. Then it was that Sir Chetwynd Lyle, with his paunch discreetly restrained within the limits of a Windsor uniform which had been made for him some two or three years since, paced up and down complacently in the moonlight, watching his two "girls," Muriel and Dolly, doing business with certain "eligibles"; then it was that Lady Fulkeward, fearfully and wonderfully got up as the "Duchess

MARIE CORELLI

of Gainsborough" sidled to and fro, flirted with this man, flouted that, giggled, shrugged her shoulders, waved her fan, and comported herself altogether as if she were a hoyden of seventeen just let loose from school for the holidays. And then the worthy Dr. Maxwell Dean, somewhat exhausted by vigorous capering in the "Lancers," strolled forth to inhale the air, fanning himself with his cap as he walked, and listening keenly to every chance word or sentence he could hear, whether it concerned himself or not. He had peculiar theories, and one of them was, as he would tell you, that if you overheard a remark apparently not intended for you, you were to make yourself quite easy, as it was "a point of predestination" that you should at that particular moment, consciously or unconsciously, play the eavesdropper. The reason of it would, he always averred, be explained to you later on in your career. The well-known saying "listeners never hear any good of themselves" was, he declared, a most ridiculous aphorism. "You overhear persons talking and you listen. Very well. It may chance that you hear yourself abused. What then? Nothing can be so good for you as such abuse; the instruction given is twofold; it warns you against foes whom you have perhaps considered friends, and it tones down any overweening conceit you may have had concerning your own importance or ability. Listen to everything if you are wise—I always do. I am an old and practised listener. And I have never listened in vain. All the information I have gained through listening, though apparently at first disconnected and unclassified, has fitted into my work like the stray pieces of a puzzle, and has proved eminently useful. Wherever I am I always keep my ears well open."

With such views as he thus entertained, life was always enormously interesting to Dr. Dean—he found nothing tiresome, not even the conversation of the type known as Noodle. The Noodle was as curious a specimen of nature to him as the emu or the crocodile. And as he turned up his intellectual little physiognomy to the deep, warm Egyptian sky and inhaled the air sniffingly, as though it were a monster scent-bottle just uncorked for his special gratification, he smiled as he observed Muriel Chetwynd Lyle standing entirely alone at the end of the terrace, attired as a "Boulogne fish-wife," and looking daggers after the hastily-retreating figure of a "White Hussar,"—no other than Ross Courtney.

"How extremely droll a 'Boulogne fish-wife' looks in Egypt," commented the Doctor to his inward self. "Remarkable! The incongruity is peculiarly typical of the Chetwynd Lyles. The costume of the young woman is like the knighthood of her father,—droll, droll, very droll!" Aloud he said—"Why are you not dancing, Miss Muriel?"

"Oh, I don't know—I'm tired," she said, petulantly. "Besides, all the men are after that Ziska woman,—they seem to have lost their heads about her!"

"Ah!" and Dr. Dean rubbed his hands. "Yes—possibly! Well, she is certainly very beautiful."

"I cannot see it!" and Muriel Chetwynd Lyle flushed with the inward rage which could not be spoken. "It's the way she dresses more than her looks. Nobody knows who she is—but they do not seem to care about that. They are all raving like lunatics over her, and that man—that artist who arrived here to-day, Armand Gervase,—seems the maddest of the lot. Haven't you noticed how often he has danced with her?"

"I couldn't help noticing that," said the Doctor, emphatically, "for I have never seen anything more exquisite than the way they waltz together. Physically, they seem made for one another."

Muriel laughed disdainfully.

"You had better tell Mr. Denzil Murray that; he is in a bad enough humor now, and that remark of yours wouldn't improve it, I can tell you!"

She broke off abruptly, as a slim, fair girl, dressed as a Greek vestal in white, with a chaplet of silver myrtle-leaves round her hair, suddenly approached and touched Dr. Dean on the arm.

"Can I speak to you a moment?" she asked.

"My dear Miss Murray! Of course!" and the Doctor turned to her at once. "What is it?"

She paced with him a few steps in silence, while Muriel Chetwynd Lyle moved languidly away from the terrace and re-entered the ball-room.

"What is it?" repeated Dr. Dean. "You seem distressed; come, tell me all about it!"

Helen Murray lifted her eyes—the soft, violet-gray eyes that Lord Fulkeward had said he admired—suffused with tears, and fixed them on the old man's face.

"I wish," she said—"I wish we had never come to Egypt! I feel as if some great misfortune were going to happen to us; I do, indeed! Oh, Dr. Dean, have you watched my brother this evening?"

"I have," he replied, and then was silent.

"And what do you think?" she asked anxiously. "How can you account for his strangeness—his roughness—even to me?"

And the tears brimmed over and fell, despite her efforts to restrain them. Dr. Dean stopped in his walk and took her two hands in his own.

"My dear Helen, it's no use worrying yourself like this," he said. "Nothing can stop the progress of the Inevitable. I have watched Denzil, I have watched the new arrival, Armand Gervase, I have watched the mysterious Ziska, and I have watched you! Well, what is the result? The Inevitable,—simply the unconquerable Inevitable. Denzil is in love, Gervase is in love, everybody is in love, except me and one other! It is a whole network of mischief, and I am the unhappy fly that has unconsciously fallen into the very middle of it. But the spider, my dear,—the spider who wove the web in the first instance,—is the Princess Ziska, and she is NOT in love! She is the other one. She is not in love with anybody any more than I am. She's got something else on her mind—I don't know what it is exactly, but it isn't love. Excluding her and myself, the whole hotel is in love—You are in love!"

Helen withdrew her hands from his grasp and a deep flush reddened her fair face.

"I!" she stammered—"Dr. Dean, you are mistaken. . ."

"Dr. Dean was never mistaken on love-matters in his life," said that self-satisfied sage complacently. "Now, my dear, don't be offended. I have known both you and your brother ever since you were left little orphan children together; if I cannot speak plainly to you, who can? You are in love, little Helen—and very unwisely, too—with the man Gervase. I have heard of him often, but I never saw him before to-night. And I don't approve of him."

Helen grew as pale as she had been rosy, and her face as the moonlight fell upon it was very sorrowful.

"He stayed with us in Scotland two summers ago," she said softly. "He was very agreeable. . ."

"Ha! No doubt! He made a sort of love to you then, I suppose. I can imagine him doing it very well! There is a nice romantic glen near your house—just where the river runs, and where I caught a fifteen-pound salmon some five years ago. Ha! Catching salmon is healthy work; much better than falling in love. No, no, Helen! Gervase is not good enough for you; you want a far better man. Has he spoken to you to-night?"

"Oh, yes! And he has danced with me."

"Ha! How often?"

"Once."

"And how many times with the Princess Ziska?"

Helen's fair head drooped, and she answered nothing. All at once the little Doctor's hand closed on her arm with a soft yet firm grip.

"Look!" he whispered.

She raised her eyes and saw two figures step out on the terrace and stand in the full moonlight,—the white Bedouin dress of the one and the glittering golden robe of the other made them easily recognizable,—they were Gervase and the Princess Ziska. Helen gave a faint, quick sigh.

"Let us go in," she said.

"Nonsense! Why should we go in? On the contrary, let us join them."

"Oh, no!" and Helen shrank visibly at the very idea. "I cannot; do not ask me! I have tried—you know I have tried—to like the Princess; but something in her—I don't know what it is—repels me. To speak truthfully, I think I am afraid of her."

"Afraid! Pooh! Why should you be afraid? It is true one doesn't often see a woman with the eyes of a vampire-bat; but there is nothing to be frightened about. I have dissected the eyes of a vampire-bat—very interesting work, very. The Princess has them—only, of course, hers are larger and finer; but there is exactly the same expression in them. I am fond of study, you know; I am studying her. What! Are you determined to run away?"

"I am engaged for this dance to Mr. Courtney," said Helen, nervously.

"Well, well! We'll resume our conversation another time," and Dr. Dean took her hand and patted it pleasantly. "Don't fret yourself about Denzil; he'll be all right. And take my advice: don't marry a Bedouin chief; marry an honest, straightforward, tender-hearted Englishman who'll take care of you, not a nondescript savage who'll desert you!"

And with a humorous and kindly smile, Dr. Dean moved off to join the two motionless and picturesque figures that stood side by side looking at the moon, while Helen, like a frightened bird suddenly released, fled precipitately back to the ball-room, where Ross Courtney was already searching for her as his partner in the next waltz.

"Upon my word," mused the Doctor, "this is a very pretty kettle of fish! The Gezireh Palace Hotel is not a hotel at all, it seems to me; it is a lunatic asylum. What with Lady Fulkeward getting herself up as twenty at the age of sixty; and Muriel and Dolly Chetwynd Lyle man-hunting with more ferocity than sportsmen hunt tigers; Helen in love, Denzil in love, Gervase in love—dear me! dear me! What a list of subjects for a student's consideration! And the Princess Ziska. . ."

He broke off his meditations abruptly, vaguely impressed by the strange solemnity of the night. An equal solemnity seemed to surround the two figures to which he now drew nigh, and as the Princess Ziska turned her eyes upon him as he came, he was, to his own vexation, aware that something indefinable disturbed his usual equanimity and gave him an unpleasant thrill.

"You are enjoying a moonlight stroll, Doctor?" she inquired.

Her veil was now cast aside in a careless fold of soft drapery over her shoulders, and her face in its ethereal delicacy of feature and brilliant coloring looked almost too beautiful to be human. Dr. Dean did not reply for a moment; he was thinking what a singular resemblance there was between Armand Gervase and one of the figures on a certain Egyptian fresco in the British Museum.

"Enjoying—er—er—a what?—a moonlight stroll? Exactly—er—yes! Pardon me, Princess, my mind often wanders, and I am afraid I am getting a little deaf as well. Yes, I find the night singularly conducive to meditation; one cannot be in a land like this under a sky like this"—and he pointed to the shining heaven—"without recalling the great histories of the past."

"I daresay they were very much like the histories of the present," said Gervase smiling.

"I should doubt that. History is what man makes it; and the character of man in the early days of civilization was, I think, more forceful, more earnest, more strong of purpose, more bent on great achievements."

"The principal achievement and glory being to kill as many of one's fellow-creatures as possible!" laughed Gervase—"Like the famous warrior, Araxes, of whom the Princess has just been telling me!"

"Araxes was great, but now Araxes is a forgotten hero," said the Princess slowly, each accent of her dulcet voice chiming on the ear like the stroke of a small silver bell. "None of the modern discoverers know anything about him yet. They have not even found his tomb; but he was buried in the Pyramids with all the honors of a king. No doubt your clever men will excavate him some day."

"I think the Pyramids have been very thoroughly explored," said Dr. Dean. "Nothing of any importance remains in them now."

The Princess arched her lovely eyebrows.

"No? Ah! I daresay you know them better than I do!" and she laughed, a laugh which was not mirthful so much as scornful.

"I am very much interested in Araxes," said Gervase then, "partly, I suppose, because he is as yet in the happy condition of being an interred mummy. Nobody has dug him up, unwound his cerements, or photographed him, and his ornaments have not been stolen. And in the second place I am interested in him because it appears he was in love with the famous dancer of his day whom the Princess represents to-night,—Charmazel. I wish I had heard the story before I came to Cairo; I would have got myself up as Araxes in person to-night."

"In order to play the lover of Charmazel?" queried the Doctor.

"Exactly!" replied Gervase with flashing eyes; "I daresay I could have acted the part."

"I should imagine you could act any part," replied the Doctor, blandly. "The role of love-making comes easily to most men."

The Princess looked at him as he spoke and smiled. The jewelled scarab, set as a brooch on her bosom, flashed luridly in the moon, and in her black eyes there was a similar lurid gleam.

"Come and talk to me," she said, laying her hand on his arm; "I am tired, and the conversation of one's ball-room partners is very banal. Monsieur Gervase would like me to dance all night, I imagine; but I am too lazy. I leave such energy to Lady Fulkeward and to all the English misses and madams. I love indolence."

"Most Russian women do, I think," observed the Doctor.

She laughed.

"But I am not Russian!"

"I know. I never thought you were," he returned composedly; "but everyone in the hotel has come to the conclusion that you are!"

"They are all wrong! What can I do to put them right?" she inquired with a fascinating little upward movement of her eyebrows.

"Nothing! Leave them in their ignorance. I shall not enlighten them, though I know your nationality."

"You do?" and a curious shadow darkened her features. "But perhaps you are wrong also!"

"I think not," said the Doctor, with gentle obstinacy. "You are an Egyptian. Born in Egypt; born OF Egypt. Pure Eastern! There is nothing Western about you. Is not it so?"

She looked at him enigmatically.

"You have made a near guess," she replied; "but you are not absolutely correct. Originally, I am of Egypt."

Dr. Dean nodded pleasantly.

"Originally,—yes. That is precisely what I mean—originally! Let me take you in to supper."

He offered his arm, but Gervase made a hasty step forward.

"Princess," he began—

She waved him off lightly.

"My dear Monsieur Gervase, we are not in the desert, where Bedouin chiefs do just as they like. We are in a modern hotel in Cairo, and all the good English mammas will be dreadfully shocked if I am seen too much with you. I have danced with you five times, remember! And I will dance with you once more before I leave. When our waltz begins, come and find me in the upper-room."

She moved away on Dr. Dean's arm, and Gervase moodily drew back and let her pass. When she had gone, he lit a cigarette and walked impatiently up and down the terrace, a heavy frown wrinkling his brows. The shadow of a man suddenly darkened the moonlight in front of him, and Denzil Murray's hand fell on his shoulder.

"Gervase," he said, huskily, "I must speak to you."

Gervase glanced him up and down, taking note of his pale face and wild eyes with a certain good-humored regret and compassion.

"Say on, my friend."

Denzil looked straight at him, biting his lips hard and clenching his hands in the effort to keep down some evidently violent emotion.

"The Princess Ziska," he began,—

Gervase smiled, and flicked the ash off his cigarette.

"The Princess Ziska," he echoed,—"Yes? What of her? She seems to be the only person talked about in Cairo. Everybody in this hotel, at any rate, begins conversation with precisely the same words as you do,—'the Princess Ziska!' Upon my life, it is very amusing!"

"It is not amusing to me," said Denzil, bitterly. "To me it is a matter of life and death." He paused, and Gervase looked at him curiously. "We've always been such good friends, Gervase," he continued, "that I should be sorry if anything came between us now, so I think it is better to make a clean breast of it and speak out plainly." Again he hesitated, his face growing still paler, then with a sudden ardent light glowing in his eyes he said—"Gervase, I love the Princess Ziska!"

Gervase threw away his cigarette and laughed aloud with a wild hilarity.

"My good boy, I am very sorry for you! Sorry, too, for myself! I deplore the position in which we are placed with all my heart and soul. It is unfortunate, but it seems inevitable. You love the Princess Ziska,—and by all the gods of Egypt and Christendom, so do I!"

IV

Denzil recoiled a step backward, then with an impulsive movement strode close up to him, his face unnaturally flushed and his eyes glittering with an evil fire.

"You—you love her! What!—in one short hour, you—who have often boasted to me of having no heart, no eyes for women except as models for your canvas,—you say now that you love a woman whom you have never seen before to-night!"

"Stop!" returned Gervase somewhat moodily, "I am not so sure about that. I HAVE seen her before, though where I cannot tell. But the fire that stirs my pulses now seems to spring from some old passion suddenly revived, and the eyes of the woman we are both mad for—well! they do not inspire holiness, my dear friend! No,—neither in you nor in me! Let us be honest with each other. There is something vile in the composition of Madame la Princesse, and it responds to something equally vile in ourselves. We shall be dragged down by the force of it,—tant pis pour nous! I am sorrier for you than for myself, for you are a good fellow, au fond; you have what the world is learning to despise—sentiment. I have none; for as I told you before, I have no heart, but I have passions—tigerish ones—which must be humored; in fact, I make it my business in life to humor them."

"Do you intend to humor them in this instance?"

"Assuredly! If I can."

"Then,—friend as you have been, you can be friend no more," said Denzil fiercely. "My God! Do you not understand? My blood is as warm as yours,—I will not yield to you one smile, one look from Ziska! No!—I will kill you first!"

Gervase looked at him calmly.

"Will you? Pauvre garcon! You are such a boy still, Denzil,—by-the-bye, how old are you? Ah, I remember now,—twenty-two. Only twenty-two, and I am thirty-eight! So in the measure of time alone, your life is more valuable to you than mine is to me. If you choose, therefore, you can kill me,—now, if you like! I have a very convenient dagger in my belt—I think it has a point—which you are welcome to use for the purpose; but, for heaven's sake, don't rant about it—do it! You can kill me—of course you can; but you cannot—mark this well, Denzil!—you cannot prevent my loving the same woman whom you

MARIE CORELLI

love. I think instead of raving about the matter here in the moonlight, which has the effect of making us look like two orthodox villains in a set stage-scene, we'd better make the best of it, and resolve to abide by the lady's choice in the matter. What say you? You have known her for many days,—I have known her for two hours. You have had the first innings, so you cannot complain."

Here he playfully unfastened the Bedouin knife which hung at his belt and offered it to Denzil, holding it delicately by the glittering blade.

"One thrust, my brave boy!" he said. "And you will stop the Ziska fever in my veins at once and forever. But, unless you deal the murderer's blow, the fever will go on increasing till it reaches its extremest height, and then. . ."

"And then?" echoed Denzil.

"Then? Oh—God only knows what then!"

Denzil thrust away the offered weapon with a movement of aversion.

"You can jest," he said. "You are always jesting. But you do not know— you cannot read the horrible thoughts in my mind. I cannot resolve their meaning even to myself. There is some truth in your light words; I feel, I know instinctively, that the woman I love has an attraction about her which is not good, but evil; yet what does that matter? Do not men sometimes love vile women?"

"Always!" replied Gervase briefly.

"Gervase, I have suffered tortures ever since I saw her face!" exclaimed the unhappy lad, his self-control suddenly giving way. "You cannot imagine what my life has been! Her eyes make me mad,—the merest touch of her hand seems to drag me away invisibly. . ."

"To perdition!" finished Gervase. "That is the usual end of the journey we men take with beautiful women."

"And now," went on Denzil, hardly heeding him, "as if my own despair were not sufficient, you must needs add to it! What evil fate, I wonder, sent you to Cairo! Of course, I have no chance with her now; you are sure to win the day. And can you wonder then that I feel as if I could kill you?"

"Oh, I wonder at nothing," said Gervase calmly, "except, perhaps, at myself. And I echo your words most feelingly,—What evil fate sent me to Cairo? I cannot tell! But here I purpose to remain. My dear Murray, don't let us quarrel if we can help it; it is such a waste of time. I am not angry with you for loving la belle Ziska,—try, therefore, not to be angry with me. Let the fair one herself decide as to our merits. My own opinion is that she cares for neither of us, and, moreover, that she never will care for any one except her fascinating self. And certainly her charms are quite enough to engross her whole attention. By the way, let me ask you, Denzil, in this headstrong passion of yours,—for it is a headstrong passion, just as mine is,—do you actually intend to make the Ziska your wife if she will have you?"

"Of course," replied Murray, with some haughtiness.

A fleeting expression of amusement flitted over Gervase's features.

"It is very honorable of you," he said, "very! My dear boy, you shall have your full chance. Because I—I would not make the Princess Madame Gervase for all the world! She is not formed for a life of domesticity—and pardon me—I cannot picture her as the contented chatelaine of your grand old Scotch castle in Ross-shire."

"Why not?"

"From an artistic point of view the idea is incongruous," said Gervase lazily. "Nevertheless, I will not interfere with your wooing."

Denzil's face brightened.

"You will not?"

"I will not—I promise! But"—and here Gervase paused, looking his young friend full in the eyes, "remember, if your chance falls to the ground—if Madame gives you your conge—if she does not consent to be a Scottish chatelaine and listen every day to the bagpipes at dinner,— you cannot expect me then to be indifferent to my own desires. She shall not be Madame Gervase,—oh, no! She shall not be asked to attend to the pot-au-feu; she shall act the role for which she has dressed to-night; she shall be another Charmazel to another Araxes, though the wild days of Egypt are no more!"

A sudden shiver ran through him as he spoke, and instinctively he drew the white folds of his picturesque garb closer about him.

"There is a chill wind sweeping in from the desert," he said, "an evil, sandy breath tasting of mummy-dust blown through the crevices of the tombs of kings. Let us go in."

Murray looked at him in a kind of dull despair.

"And what is to be done?" he asked. "I cannot answer for myself— and—from what you say, neither can you."

"My dear friend—or foe—whichever you determine to be, I can answer for myself in one particular at any rate, namely, that as I told you, I shall not ask the Princess to marry me. You, on the contrary, will do so. Bonne chance! I shall do nothing to prevent Madame from accepting

MARIE CORELLI

the honorable position you intend to offer her. And till the fiat has gone forth and the fair one has decided, we will not fly at each other's throats like wolves disputing possession of a lamb; we will assume composure, even if we have it not." He paused, and laid one hand kindly on the younger man's shoulder, "Is it agreed?"

Denzil gave a mute sign of resigned acquiescence.

"Good! I like you, Denzil; you are a charming boy! Hot-tempered and a trifle melodramatic in your loves and hatreds,—yes!—for that you might have been a Provencal instead of a Scot. Before I knew you I had a vague idea that all Scotchmen were, or needs must be, ridiculous,—I don't know why. I associated them with bagpipes, short petticoats and whisky. I had no idea of the type you so well represent,—the dark, fine eyes, the strong physique, and the impetuous disposition which suggests the South rather than the North; and to-night you look so unlike the accepted cafe chantant picture of the ever-dancing Highlander that you might in very truth be a Florentine in more points than the dress which so well becomes you. Yes,—I like you—and more than you, I like your sister. That is why I don't want to quarrel with you; I wouldn't grieve Mademoiselle Helen for the world."

Murray gave him a quick, half-angry side-glance.

"You are a strange fellow, Gervase. Two summers ago you were almost in love with Helen."

Gervase sighed.

"True. Almost. That's just it. 'Almost' is a very uncomfortable word. I have been almost in love so many times. I have never been drawn by a woman's eyes and dragged down, down,—in a mad whirlpool of sweetness and poison intermixed. I have never had my soul strangled by the coils of a woman's hair—black hair, black as night,—in the perfumed meshes of which a jewelled serpent gleams. . . I have never felt the insidious horror of a love like strong drink mounting through the blood to the brain, and there making inextricable confusion of time, space, eternity, everything, except the passion itself; never, never have I felt all this, Denzil, till to-night! To-night! Bah! It is a wild night of dancing and folly, and the Princess Ziska is to blame for it all! Don't look so tragic, my good Denzil,—what ails you now?"

"What ails me? Good Heavens! Can you ask it!" and Murray gave a gesture of mingled despair and impatience. "If you love her in this wild, uncontrolled way. . ."

"It is the only way I know of," said Gervase. "Love must be wild and uncontrolled to save it from banalite. It must be a summer thunderstorm; the heavy brooding of the clouds of thought, the lightning of desire, then the crash, the downpour,—and the end, in which the bland sun smiles upon a bland world of dull but wholesome routine and tame conventionality, making believe that there never was such a thing known as the past storm! Be consoled, Denzil, and trust me,—you shall have time to make your honorable proposal, and Madame had better accept you,—for your love would last,—mine could not!"

He spoke with a strange fierceness and irritability, and his eyes were darkened by a sudden shadow of melancholy. Denzil, bewildered at his words and manner, stared at him in a kind of helpless indignation.

"Then you admit yourself to be cruel and unprincipled?" he said.

Gervase smiled, with a little shrug of impatience.

"Do I? I was not aware of it. Is inconstancy to women cruelty and want of principle? If so, all men must bear the brunt of the accusation with me. For men were originally barbarians, and always looked upon women as toys or slaves; the barbaric taint is not out of us yet, I assure you,—at any rate, it is not out of me. I am a pure savage; I consider the love of woman as my right; if I win it, I enjoy it as long as I please, but no longer,—and not all the forces of heaven and earth should bind me to any woman I had once grown weary of."

"If that is your character," said Murray stiffly, "it were well the Princess Ziska should know it."

"True," and Gervase laughed loudly. "Tell her, man ami! Tell her that Armand Gervase is an unprincipled villain, not worth a glance from her dazzling eyes! It will be the way to make her adore me! My good boy, do you not know that there is something very marvellous in the attraction we call love? It is a pre-ordained destiny,—and if one soul is so constituted that it must meet and mix with another, nothing can hinder the operation. So that, believe me, I am quite indifferent as to what you say of me to Madame la Princesse or to anyone else. It will not be for either my looks or my character that she will love me if, indeed, she ever does love me; it will be for something indistinct, indefinable but resistless in us both, which no one on earth can explain. And now I must go, Denzil, and claim the fair one for this waltz. Try and look less miserable, my dear fellow,—I will not quarrel with you on the Princess's account, nor on any other pretext if I can help it,—for I don't want to kill you, and I am convinced your death and not mine would be the result of a fight between us!"

His eyes flashed under his straight, fierce brows with a sudden touch of imperiousness, and his commanding presence became magnetic, almost over-powering. Tormented with a dozen cross-currents of feeling, young Denzil Murray was mute;—only his breath came and went quickly, and there was a certain silently-declared antagonism in his very attitude. Gervase saw it and smiled; then turning away with his peculiarly noiseless step and grace of bearing, he disappeared.

V

Ten minutes later the larger number of dancers in the ball-room came to a sudden pause in their gyrations and stood looking on in open-mouthed, reluctantly-admiring wonderment at the exquisite waltz movements of the Princess Ziska as she floated past them in the arms of Gervase, who, as a "Bedouin chief," was perhaps only acting his part aright when he held her to him with so passionate and close a grip and gazed down upon her fair face with such a burning ardor in his eyes. Nothing in the dancing world was ever seen like the dancing of these two—nothing so languorously beautiful as the swaying grace of their well-matched figures gliding to the music in as perfectly harmonious a measure as a bird's two wings beat to the pulsations of the air. People noticed that as the Princess danced a tiny tinkling sound accompanied her every step; and the more curious observers, peeping downwards as she flew by, saw that she had kept to the details of ancient Egyptian costume so exactly that she even wore sandals, and that her feet, perfectly shaped and lovely as perfectly shaped and lovely hands, were bare save for the sandal-ribbons which crossed them, and which were fastened with jewels. Round the slim ankles were light bands of gold, also glittering with gems, and furthermore adorned by little golden bells which produced the pretty tinkling music that attracted attention.

"What a delightful creature she is!" said Lady Fulkeward, settling her "Duchess of Gainsborough" hat on her powdered wig more becomingly and smiling up in the face of Ross Courtney, who happened to be standing close by. "So sweetly unconventional! Everybody here thinks her improper; she may be, but I like her. I'm not a bit of a prude."

Courtney smiled irreverently at this. Prudery and "old" Lady Fulkeward were indeed wide apart. Aloud he said:

"I think whenever a woman is exceptionally beautiful she generally gets reported as 'improper' by her own sex; especially if she has a fascinating manner and dresses well."

"So true," and Lady Fulkeward simpered. "Exactly what I find wherever I go! Poor dear Ziska! She has to pay the penalty for captivating all you men in the way she does. I'm sure You have lost your heart to her quite as much as anybody else, haven't you?"

Courtney reddened.

"I don't think so," he answered; "I admire her very much, but I haven't lost my heart. . ."

"Naughty boy! Don't prevaricate!" and Lady Fulkeward smiled in the bewitching pearly manner her admirably-made artificial teeth allowed her to do. "Every man in the hotel is in love with the Princess, and I'm sure I don't blame them. If I belonged to your sex I should be in love with her too. As it is, I am in love with the new arrival, that glorious creature, Gervase. He is superb! He looks like an untamed savage. I adore handsome barbarians!"

"He's scarcely a barbarian, I think," said Courtney, with some amusement; "he is the great French artist, the 'lion' of Paris just now,— only secondary to Sarah Bernhardt."

"Artists are always barbarians," declared Lady Fulkeward enthusiastically. "They paint naughty people without any clothes on; they never have any idea of time; they never keep their appointments; and they are always falling in love with the wrong person and getting into trouble, which is so nice of them! That's why I worship them all. They are so refreshingly unlike Our set!"

Courtney raised his eyebrows inquiringly.

"You know what I mean by our set," went on the vivacious old "Gainsborough," "the aristocrats whose conversation is limited to the weather and scandal, and who are so frightfully dull! Dull! My dear Ross you know how dull they are!"

"Well, upon my word, they are," admitted Courtney. "You are right there. I certainly agree with you."

"I'm sure you do! They have no ideas. Now, artists have ideas,— they live on ideas and sentiment. Sentiment is such a beautiful thing—so charming! I believe that fierce-looking Gervase is a creature of sentiment—and how delightful that is! Of course, he'll paint the Princess Ziska—he Must paint her,—no one else could do it so well. By the way, have you been asked to her great party next week?"

"Yes."

"And are you going?"

"Most assuredly."

"So am I. That absurd Chetwynd Lyle woman came to me this evening and asked me if I really thought it would be proper to take her 'girls' there," and Lady Fulkeward laughed shrilly. "Girls indeed! I should say those two long, ugly women could go anywhere with safety.

'Do you consider the Princess a proper woman?' she asked, and I said, 'Certainly, as proper as you are.'"

Courtney laughed outright, and began to think there was some fun in Lady Fulkeward.

"By Jove! Did you tell her that?"

"I should think I did! Oh, I know a thing or two about the Chetwynd Lyles, but I keep my mouth shut till it suits me to open it. I said I was going, and then, of course, she said she would."

"Naturally."

And Courtney gave the answer vaguely, for the waltz was ended, and the Princess Ziska, on the arm of Gervase, was leaving the ball-room.

"She's going," exclaimed Lady Fulkeward. "Dear creature! Excuse me—I must speak to her for a moment."

And with a swish of her full skirts and a toss of her huge hat and feathers, the lively flirt of sixty tripped off with all the agility of sixteen, leaving Courtney to follow her or remain where he was, just as he chose. He hesitated, and during that undecided pause was joined by Dr. Maxwell Dean.

"A very brilliant and interesting evening!" said that individual, smiling complacently. "I don't remember any time when I have enjoyed myself so thoroughly."

"Really! I shouldn't have thought you a man to care for fancy-dress balls," said Courtney.

"Shouldn't you? Ha! Well, some fancy-dress balls I might not care for, but this one has been highly productive of entertainment in every way, and several incidents connected with it have opened up to me a new vista of research, the possibilities of which are—er—very interesting and remarkable."

"Indeed!" murmured Courtney indifferently, his eyes fixed on the slim, supple figure of the Princess Ziska as she slowly moved amid her circle of admirers out of the ball-room, her golden skirts gleaming sun-like against the polished floor, and the jewels about her flashing in vivid points of light from the hem of her robe to the snake in her hair.

"Yes," continued the Doctor, smiling and rubbing his hands, "I think I have got the clue to a very interesting problem. But I see you are absorbed—and no wonder! A charming woman, the Princess Ziska—charming! Do you believe in ghosts?"

This question was put with such unexpected abruptness that Courtney was quite taken aback.

"Ghosts?" he echoed. "No, I cannot say I do. I have never seen one, and I have never heard of one that did not turn out a bogus."

"Oh! I don't mean the usual sort of ghost," said the Doctor, drawing his shelving brows together in a meditative knot of criss-cross lines over his small, speculative eyes. "The ghost that is common to Scotch castles and English manor-houses, and that appears in an orthodox night-gown, sighs, screams, rattles chains and bangs doors ad libitum. No, no! That kind of ghost is composed of indigestion, aided by rats and a gust of wind. No; when I say ghosts, I mean ghosts—ghosts that do not need the midnight hour to evolve themselves into being, and that by no means vanish at cock-crow. My ghosts are those that move about among us in social intercourse for days, months—sometimes years— according to their several missions; ghosts that talk to us, imitate our customs and ways, shake hands with us, laugh and dance with us, and altogether comport themselves like human beings. Those are my kind of ghosts—'scientific' ghosts. There are hundreds, aye, perhaps thousands of them in the world at this very moment."

An uncomfortable shudder ran through Courtney's veins; the Doctor's manner seemed peculiar and uncanny.

"By Jove! I hope not!" he involuntarily exclaimed. "The orthodox ghost is an infinitely better arrangement. One at least knows what to expect. But a 'scientific' ghost that moves about in society, resembling ourselves in every respect, appearing to be actually human and yet having no humanity at all in its composition, is a terrific notion indeed! You don't mean to say you believe in the possibility of such an appalling creature?"

"I not only believe it," answered the Doctor composedly, "I know it!"

Here the band crashed out "God save the Queen," which, as a witty Italian once remarked, is the De Profundis of every English festivity.

"But—God bless my soul!" began Courtney. . .

"No, don't say that!" urged the Doctor. "Say 'God save the Queen.' It's more British."

"Bother 'God save the Queen,'" exclaimed Courtney impatiently.— "Look here, you don't mean it seriously, do you?"

"I always mean everything seriously," said Dr. Dean,—"even my jokes."

"Now come, no nonsense, Doctor," and Courtney, taking his arm, led him towards one of the windows opening out to the moonlit garden,— "can you, as an honest man, assure me in sober earnest that there are 'scientific ghosts' of the nature you describe?"

The little Doctor surveyed the scenery, glanced up at the moon, and then at his companion's pleasant but not very intelligent face.

"I would rather not discuss the matter," he said at last, with some brusqueness. "There are certain subjects connected with psychic phenomena on which it is best to be silent; besides, what interest can such things have for you? You are a sportsman,—keep to your big game, and leave ghost-hunting to me."

"That is not a fair answer to my question," said Courtney, "I'm sure I don't want to interfere with your researches in any way; I only want to know if it is a fact that ghosts exist, and that they are really of such a nature as to deserve the term 'scientific.'"

Dr. Dean was silent a moment. Then, stretching out his small, thin hand, he pointed to the clear sky, where the stars were almost lost to sight in the brilliance of the moon.

"Look out there!" he said, his voice thrilling with sudden and solemn fervor. "There in the limitless ether move millions of universes—vast creations which our finite brains cannot estimate without reeling,—enormous forces always at work, in the mighty movements of which our earth is nothing more than a grain of sand. Yet far more marvellous than their size or number is the mathematical exactitude of their proportions,—the minute perfection of their balance,—the exquisite precision with which every one part is fitted to another part, not a pin's point awry, not a hair's breadth astray. Well, the same exactitude which rules the formation and working of Matter controls the formation and working of Spirit; and this is why I know that ghosts exist, and, moreover, that we are COMPELLED by the laws of the phenomena surrounding us to meet them every day."

"I confess I do not follow you at all," said Courtney bewildered.

"No," and Dr. Dean smiled curiously. "I have perhaps expressed myself obscurely. Yet I am generally considered a clear exponent. First of all, let me ask you, do you believe in the existence of Matter?"

"Why, of course!"

"You do. Then you will no doubt admit that there is Something—an Intelligent Principle or Spiritual Force—which creates and controls this Matter?"

Courtney hesitated.

"Well, I suppose there must be," he said at last. "I'm not a church-goer, and I'm rather a free-thinker, but I certainly believe there is a Mind at work behind the Matter."

"That being the case," proceeded the Doctor, "I suppose you will not deny to this Invisible Mind the same exactitude of proportion and precise method of action already granted to Visible Matter?".

"Of course, I could not deny such a reasonable proposition," said Courtney.

"Very good! Pursuing the argument logically, and allowing for an exactly-moving Mind behind exactly-working Matter, it follows that there can be no such thing as injustice anywhere in the universe?"

"My dear Socrates redivivus," laughed Courtney, "I fail to see what all this has to do with ghosts."

"It has everything to do with them," declared the Doctor emphatically, "I repeat that if we grant these already stated premises concerning the composition of Mind and Matter, there can be no such thing as injustice. Yet seemingly unjust things are done every day, and seemingly go unpunished. I say 'seemingly' advisedly, because the punishment is always administered. And here the 'scientific ghosts' come in. 'Vengeance is mine,' saith the Lord,—and the ghosts I speak of are the Lord's way of doing it."

"You mean. . ." began Courtney.

"I mean," continued the Doctor with some excitement, "that the sinner who imagines his sins are undiscovered is a fool who deceives himself. I mean that the murderer who has secretly torn the life out of his shrieking victim in some unfrequented spot, and has succeeded in hiding his crime from what we call 'justice,' cannot escape the Spiritual law of vengeance. What would you say," and Dr. Dean laid his thin fingers on Courtney's coat-sleeve with a light pressure,—"if I told you that the soul of a murdered creature is often sent back to earth in human shape to dog its murderer down? And that many a criminal undiscovered by the police is haunted by a seeming Person,—a man or a woman,—who is on terms of intimacy with him,—who eats at his table, drinks his wine, clasps his hand, smiles in his face, and yet is truly nothing but the ghost of his victim in human disguise, sent to drag him gradually to his well-deserved, miserable end; what would you say to such a thing?"

"Horrible!" exclaimed Courtney, recoiling. "Beyond everything monstrous and horrible!"

The Doctor smiled and withdrew his hand from his companion's arm.

"There are a great many horrible things in the universe as well as pleasant ones," he observed dryly. "Crime and its results are always of a disagreeable nature. But we cannot alter the psychic law of equity any more than we can alter the material law of gravitation. It is growing late; I think, if you will excuse me, I will go to bed."

Courtney look at him puzzled and baffled.

"Then your 'scientific ghosts' are positive realities?" he began; here he gave a violent start as a tall white figure suddenly moved out of the shadows in the garden and came slowly towards them. "Upon my life, Doctor, you have made me quite nervous!"

"No, no, surely not," smiled the Doctor pleasantly—"not nervous! Not such a brave killer of game as you are! No, no! You don't take Monsieur Armand Gervase for a ghost, do you? He is too substantial,—far too substantial! Ha! ha! ha!"

And he laughed quietly, the wrinkled smile still remaining on his face as Gervase approached.

"Everybody is going to bed," said the great artist lazily. "With the departure of the Princess Ziska, the pleasures of the evening are ended."

"She is certainly the belle of Cairo this season," said Courtney, "but I tell you what,—I am rather sorry to see young Murray has lost his head about her."

"Parbleu! So am I," said Gervase imperturbably; "it seems a pity."

"He will get over it," interposed Dr. Dean placidly. "It's an illness,—like typhoid,—we must do all we can to keep down the temperature of the patient, and we shall pull him through."

"Keep him cool, in short!" laughed Gervase.

"Exactly!" The little Doctor smiled shrewdly. "You look feverish, Monsieur Gervase."

Gervase flushed red under his dark skin.

"I daresay I am feverish," he replied irritably,—"I find this place hot as an oven. I think I should go away to-morrow if I had not asked the Princess Ziska to sit to me."

"You are going to paint her picture?" exclaimed Courtney. "By Jove! I congratulate you. It will be the masterpiece of the next salon."

Gervase bowed.

"You flatter me! The Princess is undoubtedly an attractive subject. But, as I said before, this place stifles me. I think the hotel is too near the river,—there is an oozy smell from the Nile that I hate, and the heat is perfectly sulphureous. Don't you find it so, Doctor?"

"N-n-o! I cannot say that I do. Let me feel your pulse; I am not a medical man—but I can easily recognize any premonitions of illness."

Gervase held out his long, brown, well-shaped hand, and the savant's small, cool fingers pressed lightly on his wrist.

"You are quite well, Monsieur Gervase," he said after a pause,—"You have a little sur-excitation of the nerves, certainly,—but it is not curable by medicine." He dropped the hand he held, and looked up—"Good-night!"

"Good-night!" responded Gervase.

"Good-night!" added Courtney.

And with an amiable salutation the Doctor went his way. The ball-room was now quite deserted, and the hotel servants were extinguishing the lights.

"A curious little man, that Doctor," observed Gervase, addressing Courtney, to whom as yet he had not been formally introduced.

"Very curious!" was the reply, "I have known him for some years,—he is a very clever man, but I have never been able quite to make him out. I think he is a bit eccentric. He's just been telling me he believes in ghosts."

"Ah, poor fellow!" and Gervase yawned as, with his companion, he crossed the deserted ball-room. "Then he has what you call a screw loose. I suppose it is that which makes him interesting. Good-night!"

"Good-night!"

And separating, they went their several ways to the small, cell-like bedrooms, which are the prime discomfort of the Gezireh Palace Hotel, and soon a great silence reigned throughout the building. All Cairo slept,—save where at an open lattice window the moon shone full on a face up-turned to her silver radiance,—the white, watchful face, and dark, sleepless eyes of the Princess Ziska.

VI

N ext day the ordinary course of things was resumed at the Gezireh Palace Hotel, and the delights and flirtations of the fancy-ball began to vanish into what Hans Breitmann calls "the ewigkeit". Men were lazier than usual and came down later to breakfast, and girls looked worn and haggard with over-much dancing, but otherwise there was no sign to indicate that the festivity of the past evening had left "tracks behind," or made a lasting impression of importance on any human life. Lady Chetwynd Lyle, portly and pig-faced, sat on the terrace working at an elaborate piece of cross-stitch, talking scandal in the civilest tone imaginable, and damning all her "dear friends" with that peculiar air of entire politeness and good breeding which distinguishes certain ladies when they are saying nasty things about one another. Her daughters, Muriel and Dolly, sat dutifully near her, one reading the Daily Dial, as befitted the offspring of the editor and proprietor thereof, the other knitting. Lord Fulkeward lounged on the balustrade close by, and his lovely mother, attired in quite a charming and girlish costume of white foulard exquisitely cut and fitting into a waist not measuring more than twenty-two inches, reclined in a long deck-chair, looking the very pink of painted and powdered perfection.

"You are so very lenient," Lady Chetwynd Lyle was saying, as she bent over her needlework. "So very lenient, my dear Lady Fulkeward, that I am afraid you do not read people's characters as correctly as I do. I have had, owing to my husband's position in journalism, a great deal of social experience, and I assure you I do Not think the Princess Ziska a safe person. She may be perfectly proper—she May be—but she is not the style we are accustomed to in London."

"I should rather think not!" interrupted Lord Fulkeward, hastily. "By Jove! She wouldn't have a hair left on her head in London, don'cher know!"

"What do you mean?" inquired Muriel Chetwynd Lyle, simpering. "You really do say such funny things, Lord Fulkeward!"

"Do I?" and the young nobleman was so alarmed and embarrassed at the very idea of his ever saying funny things that he was rendered quite speechless for a moment. Anon he took heart and resumed: "Er— well—I mean that the society women would tear her to bits in no time.

She'd get asked nowhere, but she'd get blackguarded everywhere; she couldn't help herself with that face and those eyes."

His mother laughed.

"Dear Fulke! You are such a naughty boy! You shouldn't make such remarks before Lady Lyle. She never says anything against anyone!"

"Dear Fulke" stared. Had he given vent to his feelings he would have exclaimed: "Oh, Lord!—isn't the old lady a deep one!" But as it was he attended to his young moustache anxiously and remained silent. Lady Chetwynd Lyle meanwhile flushed with annoyance; she felt that Lady Fulkeward's remark was sarcastic, but she could not very well resent it, seeing that Lady Fulkeward was a peeress of the realm, and that she herself, by the strict laws of heraldry, was truly only "Dame" Chetwynd Lyle, as wife of an ordinary knight, and had no business to be called "her ladyship" at all.

"I should, indeed, be sorry," she said, primly, "if I were mistaken in my private estimate of the Princess Ziska's character, but I must believe my own eyes and the evidence of my own senses, and surely no one can condone the extremely fast way in which she behaved with that new man—that French artist, Armand Gervase—last night. Why, she danced six times with him! And she actually allowed him to walk home with her through the streets of Cairo! They went off together, in their fancy dresses, just as they were! I never heard of such a thing!"

"Oh, there was nothing remarkable at all in that," said Lord Fulkeward. "Everybody went about the place in fancy costume last night. I went out in my Neapolitan dress with a girl, and I met Denzil Murray coming down a street just behind here—took him for a Florentine prince, upon my word! And I bet you Gervase never got beyond the door of the Princess's palace; for that blessed old Nubian she keeps—the chap with a face like a mummy—bangs the gate in everybody's face, and says in guttural French: 'La Princesse ne voit per-r-r-sonne!' I've tried it. I tell you it's no go!"

"Well, we shall all get inside the mysterious palace next Wednesday evening," said Lady Fulkeward, closing her eyes with a graceful air of languor, "It will be charming, I am sure, and I daresay we shall find that there is no mystery at all about it."

"Two months ago," suddenly said a smooth voice behind them, "the Ziska's house or palace was uninhabited."

Lady Fulkeward gave a little scream and looked round.

"Good gracious, Dr. Dean! How you frightened me!"

The Doctor made an apologetic bow.

"I am very sorry. I forgot you were so sensitive; pray pardon me! As I was saying, two months ago the palace of the Princess Ziska was a deserted barrack. Formerly, so I hear, it used to be the house of some great personage; but it had been allowed to fall into decay, and nobody would rent it, even for the rush of the Cairene season, till it was secured by the Nubian you were speaking of just now—the interesting Nubian with the face like a mummy; he took it and furnished it, and when it was ready Madame la Princesse appeared on the scene and has resided there every since."

"I wonder what that Nubian has to do with her?" said Lady Chetwynd Lyle, severely.

"Nothing at all," replied the Doctor, calmly. "He is the merest servant—the kind of person who is 'told off' to attend on the women of a harem."

"Ah, I see you have been making inquiries concerning the princess, Doctor," said Lady Fulkeward, with a smile.

"I have."

"And have you found out anything about her?"

"No; that is, nothing of social importance, except, perhaps, two items—first, that she is not a Russian; secondly, that she has never been married."

"Never been married!" exclaimed Lady Chetwynd Lyle, then suddenly turning to her daughters she said blandly: "Muriel, Dolly, go into the house, my dears. It is getting rather warm for you on this terrace. I will join you in a few minutes."

The "girls" rose obediently with a delightfully innocent and juvenile air, and fortunately for them did not notice the irreverent smile that played on young Lord Fulkeward's face, which was immediately reflected on the artistically tinted countenance of his mother, at the manner of their dismissal.

"There is surely nothing improper in never having been married," said Dr. Dean, with a mock serious air. "Consider, my dear Lady Lyle, is there not something very chaste and beautiful in the aspect of an old maid?"

Lady Lyle looked up sharply. She had an idea that both she and her daughters were being quizzed, and she had some difficulty to control her rising temper.

"Then do you call the Princess an old maid?" she demanded.

Lady Fulkeward looked amused; her son laughed outright. But the Doctor's face was perfectly composed.

"I don't know what else I can call her," he said, with a thoughtful air. "She is no longer in her teens, and she has too much voluptuous charm for an ingenue. Still, I admit, you would scarcely call her 'old' except in the parlance of the modern matrimonial market. Our present-day roues, you know, prefer their victims young, and I fancy the Princess Ziska would be too old and perhaps too clever for most of them. Personally speaking, she does not impress me as being of any particular age, but as she is not married, and is, so to speak, a maid fully developed, I am perforce obliged to call her an old maid."

"She wouldn't thank you for the compliment," said Lady Lyle with a spiteful grin.

"I daresay not," responded the Doctor blandly, "but I imagine she has very little personal vanity. Her mind is too preoccupied with something more important than the consideration of her own good looks."

"And what is that?" inquired Lady Fulkeward, with some curiosity.

"Ah! there is the difficulty! What is it that engrosses our fair friend more than the looking-glass? I should like to know—but I cannot find out. It is an enigma as profound as that of the sphinx. Good-morning, Monsieur Gervase!"—and, turning round, he addressed the artist, who just then stepped out on the terrace carrying a paintbox and a large canvas strapped together in portable form. "Are you going to sketch some picturesque corner of the city?"

"No," replied Gervase, listlessly raising his white sun-hat to the ladies present with a courteous, yet somewhat indifferent grace. "I'm going to the Princess Ziska's. I shall probably get the whole outline of her features this morning."

"A full-length portrait?" inquired the Doctor.

"I fancy not. Not the first attempt, at any rate—head and shoulders only."

"Do you know where her house is?" asked Lord Fulkeward. "If you don't, I'll walk with you and show you the way."

"Thanks—you are very good. I shall be obliged to you."

And raising his hat again he sauntered slowly off, young Fulkeward walking with him and chatting to him with more animation than that exhausted and somewhat vacant-minded aristocrat usually showed to anyone.

"It is exceedingly warm," said Lady Lyle, rising then and putting away her cross-stitch apparatus, "I thought of driving to the Pyramids this afternoon, but really. . ."

"There is shade all the way," suggested the Doctor, "I said as much to a young woman this morning who has been in the hotel for nearly two months, and hasn't seen the Pyramids yet."

"What has she been doing with herself?" asked Lady Fulkeward, smiling.

"Dancing with officers," said Dr. Dean. "How can Cheops compare with a moustached noodle in military uniform! Good-bye for the present; I'm going to hunt for scarabei."

"I thought you had such a collection of them already," said Lady Lyle.

"So I have. But the Princess had a remarkable one on last night, and I want to find another like it. It's blue—very blue—almost like a rare turquoise, and it appears it is the sign-manual of the warrior Araxes, who was a kind of king in his way, or desert chief, which was about the same thing in those days. He fought for Amenhotep, and seemed from all accounts to be a greater man than Amenhotep himself. The Princess Ziska is a wonderful Egyptologist; I had a most interesting conversation with her last night in the supper-room."

"Then she is really a woman of culture and intelligence?" queried Lady Lyle.

The Doctor smiled.

"I should say she would be a great deal too much for the University of Oxford, as far as Oriental learning goes," he said. "She can read the Egyptian papyri, she tells me, and she can decipher anything on any of the monuments. I only wish I could persuade her to accompany me to Thebes and Karnak."

Lady Fulkeward unfurled her fan and swayed it to and fro with an elegant languor.

"How delightful that would be!" she sighed. "So romantic and solemn—all those dear old cities with those marvellous figures of the Egyptians carved and painted on the stones! And Rameses—dear Rameses! He really has good legs everywhere! Haven't you noticed that? So many of these ancient sculptures represent the Egyptians with such angular bodies and such frightfully thin legs, but Rameses always has good legs wherever you find him. It's so refreshing! Do make up a party, Dr. Dean!—we'll all go with you; and I'm sure the Princess Ziska will be the most charming companion possible. Let us have a dahabeah! I'm good for half the expenses, if you will only arrange everything."

The Doctor stroked his chin and looked dubious, but he was evidently attracted by the idea.

"I'll see about it," he said at last. "Meanwhile I'll go and have a hunt for some traces of Amenhotep and Araxes."

He strolled down the terrace, and Lady Chetwynd Lyle, turning her back on "old" Lady Fulkeward, went after her "girls," while the fascinating Fulkeward herself continued to recline comfortably in her chair, and presently smiled a welcome on a youngish-looking man with a fair moustache who came forward and sat down beside her, talking to her in low, tender and confidential tones. He was the very impecunious colonel of one of the regiments then stationed in Cairo, and as he never wasted time on sentiment, he had been lately thinking that a marriage with a widowed peeress who had twenty thousand pounds a year in her own right might not be a "half bad" arrangement for him. So he determined to do the agreeable, and as he was a perfect adept in the art of making love without feeling it, he got on very well, and his prospects brightened steadily hour by hour.

Meanwhile young Fulkeward was escorting Armand Gervase through several narrow by-streets, talking to him as well as he knew how and trying in his feeble way to "draw him out," in which task he met with but indifferent success.

"It must be awfully jolly and—er—all that sort of thing to be so famous," he observed, glancing up at the strong, dark, brooding face above him. "They had a picture of yours over in London once; I went to see it with my mother. It was called 'Le Poignard,' do you remember it?"

Gervase shrugged his shoulders carelessly.

"Yes, I remember. A poor thing at its best. It was a woman with a dagger in her hand."

"Yes, awfully fine, don'cher know! She was a very dark woman—too dark for my taste,—and she'd got a poignard clasped in in her right hand. Of course, she was going to murder somebody with it; that was plain enough. You meant it so, didn't you?"

"I suppose I did."

"She was in a sort of Eastern get-up," pursued Fulkeward, "one of your former studies in Egypt, perhaps."

Gervase started, and passed his hand across his forehead with a bewildered air.

"No, no! Not a former study, by any means. How could it be? This is my first visit to Egypt. I have never been here before."

"Haven't you? Really! Well, you'll find it awfully interesting and all that sort of thing. I don't see half as much of it as I should like. I'm a weak chap—got something wrong with my lungs,—awful bother, but can't be helped. My mother won't let me do too much. Here we are; this is the Princess Ziska's."

They were standing in a narrow street ending in a cul-de-sac, with tall houses on each side which cast long, black, melancholy shadows on the rough pavement below. A vague sense of gloom and oppression stole over Gervase as he surveyed the outside of the particular dwelling Fulkeward pointed out to him—a square, palatial building, which had no doubt once been magnificent in its exterior adornment, but which now, owing to long neglect, had fallen into somewhat melancholy decay. The sombre portal, fantastically ornamented with designs copied from some of the Egyptian monuments, rather resembled the gateway of a tomb than an entrance to the private residence of a beautiful living woman, and Fulkeward, noting his companion's silence, added:

"Not a very cheerful corner, is it? Some of these places are regular holes, don'cher know; but I daresay it's all right inside."

"You have never been inside?"

"Never." And Fulkeward lowered his voice: "Look up there; there's the beast that keeps everybody out!"

Gervase followed his glance, and perceived behind the projecting carved lattice-work of one of the windows a dark, wrinkled face and two gleaming eyes which, even at that distance, had, or appeared to have, a somewhat sinister expression.

"He's the nastiest type of Nubian I have ever seen," pursued Fulkeward. "Looks just like a galvanized corpse."

Gervase smiled, and perceiving a long bell-handle at the gateway, pulled it sharply. In another moment the Nubian appeared, his aspect fully justifying Lord Fulkeward's description of him. The parchment-like skin on his face was yellowish-black, and wrinkled in a thousand places; his lips were of a livid blue, and were drawn up and down above and below the teeth in a kind of fixed grin, while the dense brilliance of his eyes was so fierce and fiery as to suggest those of some savage beast athirst for prey.

"Madame la Princesse Ziska" began Gervase, addressing his unfascinating object with apparent indifference to his hideousness.

The Nubian's grinning lips stretched themselves wider apart as, in a thick, snarling voice he demanded:

"Votre nom?"

"Armand Gervase."

"Entrez!"

"Et moi?" queried Fulkeward, with a conciliatory smile.

"Non! Pas vous. Monsieur Armand Gervase, seul!"

Fulkeward gave a resigned shrug of his shoulders; Gervase looked round at him ere he crossed the threshold of the mysterious habitation.

"I'm sorry you have to walk back alone."

"Don't mention it," said Fulkeward affably. "You see, you have come on business. You're going to paint the Princess's picture; and I daresay this blessed old rascal knows that I want nothing except to look at his mistress and wonder what she's made of."

"What she's made of?" echoed Gervase in surprise. "Don't you think she's made like other women?"

"No; can't say I do. She seems all fire and vapor and eyes in the middle, don'cher know. Oh, I'm an ass—always was—but that's the feeling she gives me. Ta-ta! Wish you a pleasant morning!"

He nodded and strolled away, and Gervase hesitated yet another moment, looking full at the Nubian, who returned him stare for stare.

"Maintenant?" he began.

"Oui, maintenant," echoed the Nubian.

"La Princesse, ou est elle?"

"La!" and the Nubian pointed down a long, dark passage beyond which there seemed to be the glimmer of green palms and other foliage. "Elle vous attend, Monsieur Armand Gervase! Entrez! Suivez!"

Slowly Gervase passed in, and the great tomb-like door closed upon him with a heavy clang. The whole long, bright day passed, and he did not reappear; not a human foot crossed the lonely street and nothing was seen there all through the warm sunshiny hours save the long, black shadows on the pavement, which grew longer and darker as the evening fell.

VII

Within the palace of the Princess Ziska a strange silence reigned. In whatever way the business of her household was carried on, it was evidently with the most absolute noiselessness, for not a sound disturbed the utter stillness environing her. She herself, clad in white garments that clung about her closely, displaying the perfect outlines of her form, stood waiting for her guest in a room that was fairly dazzling to the eye in its profusion of exquisitely assorted and harmonized colors, as well as impressive to the mind in its suggestions of the past rather than of the present. Quaint musical instruments of the fashion of thousands of years ago hung on the walls or lay on brackets and tables, but no books such as our modern time produces were to be seen; only tied-up bundles of papyri and curious little tablets of clay inscribed with mysterious hieroglyphs. Flowers adorned every corner—many of them strange blossoms which a connoisseur would have declared to be unknown in Egypt,—palms and ferns and foliage of every description were banked up against the walls in graceful profusion, and from the latticed windows the light filtered through colored squares, giving a kind of rainbow-effect to the room, as though it were a scene in a dream rather than a reality. And even more dream-like than her surroundings was the woman who awaited the approach of her visitor, her eyes turned towards the door—fiery eyes filled with such ardent watchfulness as seemed to burn the very air. The eyes of a hawk gleaming on its prey,—the eyes of a famished tiger in the dark, were less fraught with terrific meaning than the eyes of Ziska as she listened attentively to the on-coming footsteps through the outside corridor which told her that Gervase was near.

"At last!" she whispered, "at last!" The next moment the Nubian flung the door wide open and announced "Monsieur Armand Gervase!"

She advanced with all the wonderful grace which distinguished her, holding out both her slim, soft hands. Gervase caught them in his own and kissed them fervently, whereupon the Nubian retired, closing the door after him.

"You are very welcome, Monsieur Gervase," said the Princess then, speaking with a measured slowness that was attractive as well as soothing to the ear. "You have left all the dear English people well at the Gezireh Palace? Lady Fulkeward was not too tired after her exertions at the ball? And you?"

But Gervase was gazing at her in a speechless confusion of mind too great for words. A sudden, inexplicable emotion took possession of him,—an emotion to which he could give no name, but which stupefied him and held him mute. Was it her beauty which so dazzled his senses? Was it some subtle perfume in the room that awoke a dim haunting memory? Or what was it that seemed so strangely familiar? He struggled with himself, and finally spoke out his thought:

"I have seen you before, Princess; I am quite sure I have! I thought I had last night; but to-day I am positive about it. Strange, isn't it? I wonder where we really met?"

Her dark eyes rested on him fully.

"I wonder!" she echoed, smiling. "The world is so small, and so many people nowadays make the 'grand tour,' that it is not at all surprising we should have passed each other en route through our journey of life."

Gervase still hesitated, glancing about him with a singularly embarrassed air, while she continued to watch him intently. Presently his sensations, whatever they were, passed off, and gradually recovering his equanimity, he became aware that he was quite alone with one of the most fascinating women he had ever seen. His eyes flashed, and he smiled.

"I have come to paint your picture," he said softly. "Shall I begin?"

She had seated herself on a silken divan, and her head rested against a pile of richly-embroidered cushions. Without waiting for her answer, he threw himself down beside her and caught her hand in his.

"Shall I paint your picture?" he whispered. "Or shall I make love to you?"

She laughed,—the sweet, low laugh that somehow chilled his blood while it charmed his hearing.

"Whichever you please," she answered. "Both performances would no doubt be works of art!"

"What do you mean?"

"Can you not understand? If you paint my picture it will be a work of art. If you make love to me it will equally be a work of art: that is, a composed thing—an elaborate study."

"Bah! Love is not a composed thing," said Gervase, leaning closer to her. "It is wild, and full of libertinage as the sea."

"And equally as fickle," added the Princess composedly, taking a fan of feathers near her and waving it to and fro. "Man's idea of love is to take all he can get from a woman, and give her nothing in return but misery sometimes, and sometimes death."

"You do not,—you cannot think that!" said Gervase, looking at her dazzling face with a passion of admiration he made no attempt to conceal. "Men on the whole are not as cruel or as treacherous as women. I would swear, looking at you, that, beautiful as you are, you are cruel, and that is perhaps why I love you! You are like a splendid tigress waiting to be tamed!"

"And you think you could tame me?" interposed Ziska, looking at him with an inscrutable disdain in her black eyes.

"Yes, if you loved me!"

"Ah, possibly! But then it happens that I do not love you. I love no one. I have had too much of love; it is a folly I have grown weary of!"

Gervase fixed his eyes on her with an audacious look which seemed to hint that he might possibly take advantage of being alone with her to enforce his ideas of love more eloquently than was in accordance with the proprieties. She perceived his humor, smiled, and coldly gave him back glance for glance. Then, rising from the divan, she drew herself up to her full height and surveyed him with a kind of indulgent contempt.

"You are an unprincipled man, Armand Gervase," she said; "and do you know I fear you always will be! A cleansing of your soul through centuries of fire will be necessary for you in the next world,—that next world which you do not believe in. But it is perhaps as well to warn you that I am not without protection in this place. . . See!" and as she spoke she clapped her hands.

A clanging noise as of brazen bells answered her,—and Gervase, springing up from his seat, saw, to his utter amazement, the apparently solid walls of the room in which they were, divide rapidly and form themselves in several square openings which showed a much larger and vaster apartment beyond, resembling a great hall. Here were assembled some twenty or thirty gorgeously-costumed Arab attendants,—men of a dark and sinister type, who appeared to be fully armed, judging from the unpleasant-looking daggers and other weapons they carried at their belts. The Princess clapped her hands again, and the walls closed in the same rapid fashion as they had opened, while the beautiful mistress of this strange habitation laughed mirthfully at the complete confusion of her visitor and would-be lover.

"Paint me now!" she said, flinging herself in a picturesque attitude on one of the sofas close by; "I am ready."

"But *I* am not ready!" retorted Gervase, angrily. "Do you take me for a child, or a fool?"

"Both in one," responded the Princess, tranquilly; "being a man!"

His breath came and went quickly.

"Take care, beautiful Ziska!" he said. "Take care how you defy me!"

"And take care, Monsieur Gervase; take care how you defy Me!" she responded, with a strange, quick glance at him. "Do you not realize what folly you are talking? You are making love to me in the fashion of a brigand, rather than a nineteenth-century Frenchman of good standing,—and I—I have to defend myself against you also brigand-wise, by showing you that I have armed servants within call! It is very strange,—it would frighten even Lady Fulkeward, and I think she is not easily frightened. Pray commence your work, and leave such an out-of-date matter as love to dreamers and pretty sentimentalists, like Miss Helen Murray."

He was silent, and busied himself in unstrapping his canvas and paint-box with a great deal of almost vicious energy. In a few moments he had gained sufficient composure to look full at her, and taking his palette in hand, he began dabbing on the colors, talking between whiles.

"Do you suppose," he said, keeping his voice carefully subdued, "that you can intimidate me by showing me a score of wretched black rascals whom you have placed on guard to defend you out there? And why did you place them on guard? You must have been afraid of me! Pardieu! I could snatch you out of their midst, if I chose! You do not know me; if you did, you would understand that not all the world, armed to the teeth should balk me of my desires! But I have been too hasty—that I own,—I can wait." He raised his eyes and saw that she was listening with an air of amused indifference. "I shall have to mix strange tints in your portrait, ma belle! It is difficult to find the exact hue of your skin—there is rose and brown in it; and there is yet another color which I must evolve while working,—and it is not the hue of health. It is something dark and suggestive of death; I hope you are not destined to an early grave! And yet, why not? It is better that a beautiful woman should die in her beauty than live to become old and tiresome. . ."

"You think that?" interrupted the Ziska suddenly, smiling somewhat coldly.

"I do, most honestly. Had I lived in the early days of civilization, when men were allowed to have as many women as they could provide for, I would have mercifully killed any sweet favorite as soon as her beauty began to wane. A lovely woman, dead in her first exquisite youth,—how beautiful a subject for the mind to dwell upon! How it suggests all manner of poetic fancies and graceful threnodies! But a woman grown old, who has outlived all passion and is a mere bundle of fat, or a mummy of skin and bone,—what poetry does her existence suggest? How can she appeal to art or sentiment? She is a misery to herself and an eyesore to others. Yes, Princess, believe me,—Love first, and Death afterwards, are woman's best friends."

"You believe in Death?" ask the Princess, looking steadily at him.

"It is the only thing I do believe in," he answered lightly. "It is a fact that will bear examination, but not contradiction. May I ask you to turn your head slightly to the left—so! Yes, that will do; if I can catch the look in your eyes that gleams there now,—the look of intense, burning, greedy cruelty which is so murderously fascinating, I shall be content."

He seated himself opposite to her, and, putting down his palette, took up his canvas, and posing it on his knee, began drawing the first rough outline of his sketch in charcoal. She, meanwhile, leaning against heaped-up cushions of amber satin, remained silent.

"You are not a vain woman," he pursued, "or you would resent my description of your eyes. 'Greedy cruelty' is not a pretty expression, nor would it be considered complimentary by the majority of the fair sex. Yet, from my point of view, it is the highest flattery I can pay you, for I adore the eyes of savage animals, and the beautiful eye of the forest-beast is in your head,—diableresse charmante comme vous etes! I wonder what gives you such an insatiate love of vengeance?"

He looked up and saw her eyes glistening and narrowing at the corners, like the eyes of an angry snake.

"If I have such a feeling," she replied slowly, "it is probably a question of heritage."

"Ah! Your parents were perhaps barbaric in their notions of love and hatred?" he queried, lazily working at his charcoal sketch with growing admiration for its result.

"My parents came of a race of kings!" she answered. "All my ancestors were proud, and of a temper unknown to this petty day. They resented a wrong, they punished falsehood and treachery, and they took a life for a life. Your generation tolerates every sin known in the calendar with a smile and a shrug,—you have arrived at the end of your civilization, even to the denial of Deity and a future life."

"That is not the end of our civilization, Princess," said Gervase, working away intently, with eyes fixed on the canvas as he talked. "That is the triumphal apex, the glory, the culmination of everything that is great and supreme in manhood. In France, man now knows himself to be the only God; England—good, slow-pacing England—is approaching France in intelligence by degrees, and I rejoice to see that it is possible for a newspaper like the Agnostic to exist in London. Only the other day that excellent journal was discussing the possibility of teaching monkeys to read, and a witty writer, who adopts the nom de plume of 'Saladin,' very cleverly remarked 'that supposing monkeys were able to read the New Testament, they would still remain monkeys; in fact, they would probably be greater monkeys than ever.' The fact of such an expression being allowed to pass muster in once pious London is an excellent sign of the times and of our progress towards the pure Age of Reason. The name of Christ is no longer one to conjure with."

A dead silence followed his words, and the peculiar stillness and heaviness of the atmosphere struck him with a vague alarm. He lifted his eyes,—the Princess Ziska met his gaze steadily, but there was something in her aspect that moved him to wonderment and a curious touch of terror. The delicate rose-tint of her cheeks had faded to an ashy paleness, her lips were pressed together tightly and her eyes seemed to have gained a vivid and angry lustre which Medusa herself might have envied.

"Did you ever try to conjure with that name?" she asked.

"Never," he replied, forcing a smile and remonstrating with himself for the inexplicable nature of his emotions.

She went on slowly:

"In my creed—for I have a creed—it is believed that those who have never taken the sacred name of Christ to their hearts, as a talisman of comfort and support, are left as it were in the vortex of uncertainties, tossed to and fro among many whirling and mighty forces, and haunted forever by the phantoms of their own evil deeds. Till they learn and accept the truth of their marvellous Redemption, they are the prey of wicked spirits who tempt and lead them on to divers miseries. But when the great Name of Him who died upon the Cross is acknowledged, then it is found to be of that transfiguring nature which turns evil to good, and sometimes makes angels out of fiends. Nevertheless, for the hardened reprobate and unbeliever the old laws suffice."

Gervase had stopped the quick movement of his "fusin," and looked at her curiously.

"What old laws?" he asked.

"Stern justice without mercy!" she answered; then in lighter accents she added: "Have you finished your first outline?"

In reply, he turned his canvas round to her, showing her a head and profile boldly presented in black and white. She smiled.

"It is clever; but it is not like me," she said. "When you begin the coloring you will find that your picture and I have no resemblance to each other."

He flushed with a sense of wounded amour propre.

"Pardon, madame!—I am no novice at the art of painting," he said; "and much as your charms dazzle and ensnare me, they do not disqualify my brain and hand from perfectly delineating them upon my canvas. I love you to distraction; but my passion shall not hinder me from making your picture a masterpiece."

She laughed.

"What an egoist you are, Monsieur Gervase!" she said. "Even in your professed passion for me you count yourself first,—me afterwards!"

"Naturally!" he replied. "A man must always be first by natural creation. When he allows himself to play second fiddle, he is a fool!"

"And when he is a fool—and he often is—he is the first of fools!" said the Princess. "No ape—no baboon hanging by its tail to a tree—looks such a fool as a man-fool. For a man-fool has had all the opportunities of education and learning bestowed upon him; this great universe, with its daily lessons of the natural and the supernatural, is his book laid open for his reading, and when he will neither read it nor consider it, and, moreover, when he utterly denies the very Maker of it, then there is no fool in all creation like him. For the ape-fool does at least admit that there may be a stronger beast somewhere,—a creature who may suddenly come upon him and end his joys of hanging by his tail to a tree and make havoc of his fruit-eating and chattering, while man thinks there is nothing anywhere superior to himself."

Gervase smiled tolerantly.

"I am afraid I have ruffled you, Princess," he said. "I see you have religious ideas: I have none."

Once again she laughed musically.

"Religious ideas! I! Not at all. I have a creed as I told you, but it is an ugly one—not at all sentimental or agreeable. It is one I have adopted from ancient Egypt."

"Explain it to me," said Gervase; "I will adopt it also, for your sake."

"It is too supernatural for you," she said, paying no heed to the amorous tone of his voice or the expressive tenderness of his eyes.

"Never mind! Love will make me accept an army of ghosts, if necessary."

"One of the chief tenets of my faith," she continued, "is the eternal immortality of each individual Soul. Will you accept that?"

"For the moment, certainly!"

Her eyes glowed like great jewels as she proceeded:

"The Egyptian cult I follow is very briefly explained. The Soul begins in protoplasm without conscious individuality. It progresses through various forms till individual consciousness is attained. Once attained, it is never lost, but it lives on, pressing towards perfection, taking upon itself various phases of existence according to the passions which have most completely dominated it from the first. That is all. But according to this theory, you might have lived in the world long ago, and so might I: we might even have met; and for some reason or other we may have become re-incarnated now. A disciple of my creed would give you that as the reason why you sometimes imagine you have seen me before."

As she spoke, the dazed and troubled sensation he had once previously experienced came upon him; he laid down the canvas he held and passed his hand across his forehead bewilderedly.

"Yes; very curious and fantastic. I've heard a great deal about the doctrine of reincarnation. I don't believe in it,—I can't believe in it! But if I could: if I could imagine I had ever met you in some bygone time, and you were like what you are at this moment, I should have loved you,—I Must have loved you! You see I cannot leave the subject of love alone; and your re-incarnation idea gives my fancy something to work upon. So, beautiful Ziska, if your soul ever took the form of a flower, I must have been its companion blossom; if it ever paced the forest as a beast of prey, I must have been its mate; if it ever was human before, then I must have been its lover! Do you like such pretty follies? I will talk them by the hour."

Here he rose, and with a movement that was half fierce and half tender, he knelt beside her, taking her hands in his own.

"I love you, Ziska! I cannot help myself. I am drawn to you by some force stronger than my own will; but you need not be afraid of me—not yet! As I said, I can wait. I can endure the mingled torture and rapture of this sudden passion and make no sign, till my patience tires, and then—then I will win you if I die for it!"

He sprang up before she could speak a word in answer, and seizing his canvas again, exclaimed gayly:

"Now for the hues of morning and evening combined, to paint the radiance of this wicked soul of love that so enthralls me! First, the raven-black of midnight for the hair,—the lustre of the coldest, brightest stars for eyes,—the blush-rose of early dawn for lips and cheeks. Ah! How shall I make a real beginning of this marvel?"

"It will be difficult, I fear," said Ziska slowly, with a faint, cold smile; "and still more difficult, perchance, will be the end!"

VIII

The table d'hote at the Gezireh Palace Hotel had already begun when Gervase entered the dining-room and sat down near Lady Fulkeward and Dr. Dean.

"You have missed the soup," said her ladyship, looking up at him with a sweet smile. "All you artists are alike,—you have no idea whatever of time. And how have you succeeded with that charming mysterious person, the Princess Ziska?"

Gervase kept his gaze steadily fixed on the table-cloth. He was extremely pale, and had the air of one who has gone through some great mental exhaustion.

"I have not succeeded as well as I expected," he answered slowly. "I think my hand must have lost its cunning. At any rate, whatever the reason may be, Art has been defeated by Nature."

He crumbled up the piece of bread near his plate in small portions with a kind of involuntary violence in the action, and Dr. Dean, deliberately drawing out a pair of spectacles from their case, adjusted them, and surveyed him curiously.

"You mean to say that you cannot paint the Princess's picture?"

Gervase glanced up at him with a half-sullen, half-defiant expression.

"I don't say that," he replied; "I can paint something—something which you can call a picture if you like,—but there is no resemblance to the Princess Ziska in it. She is beautiful, and I can get nothing of her beauty,—I can only get the reflection of a face which is not hers."

"How very curious!" exclaimed Lady Fulkeward. "Quite psychological, is it not, Doctor? It is almost creepy!" and she managed to produce a delicate shudder of her white shoulders without cracking the blanc de perle enamel. "It will be something fresh for you to study."

"Possibly it will—possibly," said the Doctor, still surveying Gervase blandly through his round glasses; "but it isn't the first time I have heard of painters who unconsciously produce other faces than those of their sitters. I distinctly remember a case in point. A gentleman, famous for his charities and general benevolence, had his portrait painted by a great artist for presentation to the town-hall of his native place, and the artist was quite unable to avoid making him unto the likeness of a villain. It was quite a distressing affair; the painter was probably more distressed than anybody about it, and he tried by every possible means in his power to impart a truthful and noble aspect to the countenance of the man who was known and admitted to be a benefactor to his race. But it was all in vain: the portrait when finished was the portrait of a stranger and a scoundrel. The people for whom it was intended declared they would not have such a libel on their generous friend hung up in their town-hall. The painter was in despair, and there was going to be a general hubbub, when, lo and behold the 'noble' personage himself was suddenly arrested for a brutal murder committed twelve years back. He was found guilty and hanged, and the painter kept the portrait that had so remarkably betrayed the murderer's real nature, as a curiosity ever afterwards."

"Is that a fact?" inquired a man who was seated at the other side of the table, and who had listened with great interest to the story.

"A positive fact," said the Doctor. "One of those many singular circumstances which occur in life, and which are beyond all explanation."

Gervase moved restlessly; then filling for himself a glass of claret, drained it off thirstily.

"Something of the same kind has happened to me," he said with a hard, mirthless laugh, "for out of the most perfect beauty I have only succeeded in presenting an atrocity."

"Dear me!" exclaimed Lady Fulkeward. "What a disappointing day you must have had! But of course, you will try again; the Princess will surely give you another sitting?"

"Oh, yes! I shall certainly try again and yet again, and ever so many times again," said Gervase, with a kind of angry obstinacy in his tone, "the more so as she has told me I will never succeed in painting her."

"She told you that, did she?" put in Dr. Dean, with an air of lively interest.

"Yes."

Just then the handing round of fresh dishes and the clatter of knives and forks effectually put a stop to the conversation for the time, and Gervase presently glancing about him saw that Denzil Murray and his sister were dining apart at a smaller table with young Lord Fulkeward and Ross Courtney. Helen was looking her fairest and best that evening—her sweet face, framed in its angel aureole of bright hair had a singular look of pureness and truth expressed upon it rare to find in any woman beyond her early teens. Unconsciously to himself, Gervase sighed as he caught a view of her delicate profile, and Lady Fulkeward's sharp ears heard the sound of that sigh.

"Isn't that a charming little party over there?" she asked. "Young people, you know! They always like to be together! That very sweet girl, Miss Murray, was so much distressed about her brother to-day,—something was the matter with him—a touch of fever, I believe,—that she begged me to let Fulke dine with them in order to distract Mr. Denzil's mind. Fulke is a dear boy, you know—very consoling in his ways, though he says so little. Then Mr. Courtney volunteered to join them, and there they are. The Chetwynd Lyles are gone to a big dinner at the Continental this evening."

"The Chetwynd Lyles—let me see. Who are they?" mused Gervase aloud, "Do I know them?"

"No,—that is, you have not been formally introduced," said Dr. Dean. "Sir Chetwynd Lyle is the editor and proprietor of the London Daily Dial, Lady Chetwynd Lyle is his wife, and the two elderly-youthful ladies who appeared as 'Boulogne fishwives' last night at the ball are his daughters."

"Cruel man!" exclaimed Lady Fulkeward with a girlish giggle. "The idea of calling those sweet girls, Muriel and Dolly, 'elderly-youthful!'"

"What are they, my dear madam, what are they?" demanded the imperturbable little savant. "'Elderly-youthful' is a very convenient expression, and applies perfectly to people who refuse to be old and cannot possibly be young."

"Nonsense! I will not listen to you!" and her ladyship opened her jewelled fan and spread it before her eyes to completely screen the objectionable Doctor from view. "Don't you know your theories are quite out of date? Nobody is old,—we all utterly refuse to be old! Why," and she shut her fan with a sudden jerk, "I shall have you calling ME old next."

"Never, madam!" said Dr. Dean gallantly laying his hand upon his heart. "You are quite an exception to the rule. You have passed through the furnace of marriage and come out unscathed. Time has done its worst with you, and now retreats, baffled and powerless; it can touch you no more!"

Whether this was meant as a compliment or the reverse it would have been difficult to say, but Lady Fulkeward graciously accepted it as the choicest flattery, and bowed, smiling and gratified. Dinner was now drawing to its end, and people were giving their orders for coffee to be served to them on the terrace and in the gardens, Gervase among the rest. The Doctor turned to him.

"I should like to see your picture of the Princess," he said,—"that is if you have no objection."

"Not the least in the world," replied Gervase,—"only it isn't the Princess, it is somebody else."

A faint shudder passed over him. The Doctor noticed it.

"Talking of curious things," went on that irrepressible savant, "I started hunting for a particular scarabeus to-day. I couldn't find it, of course,—it generally takes years to find even a trifle that one especially wants. But I came across a queer old man in one of the curiosity-shops who told me that over at Karnak they had just discovered a large fresco in one of the tombs describing the exploits of the very man whose track I'm on—Araxes. . ."

Gervase started,—he knew not why.

"What has Araxes to do with you?" he demanded.

"Oh, nothing! But the Princess Ziska spoke of him as a great warrior in the days of Amenhotep,—and she seems to be a great Egyptologist, and to know many things of which we are ignorant. Then you know last night she adopted the costume of a dancer of that period, named Ziska-Charmazel. Well, now it appears that in one part of this fresco the scene depicted is this very Ziska-Charmazel dancing before Araxes."

Gervase listened with strained attention,—his heart beat thickly, as though the Doctor were telling him of some horrible circumstance in which he had an active part; whereas he had truly no interest at all in the matter, except in so far as events of history are more or less interesting to everyone.

"Well?" he said after a pause.

"Well," echoed Dr. Dean. "There is really nothing more to say beyond that I want to find out everything I can concerning this Araxes, if only for the reason that the charming Princess chose to impersonate his lady-love last night. One must amuse one's self in one's own fashion, even in Egypt, and this amuses ME."

Gervase rose, feeling in his pocket for his cigarette-case.

"Come," he said briefly, "I will show you my picture."

He straightened his tall, fine figure and walked slowly across the room to the table where Denzil Murray sat with his sister and friends.

"Denzil," he said,—"I have made a strange portrait of the Princess Ziska, and I'm going to show it to Dr. Dean. I should like you to see it too. Will you come?"

Denzil looked at him with a dark reproach in his eyes.

"If you like," he answered shortly.

"I do like!" and Gervase laid his hand on the young fellow's shoulder with a kind pressure. "You will find it a piece of curious disenchantment, as well as a proof of my want of skill. You are all welcome to come and look at it except. . ." here he hesitated,—"except Miss Murray. I think— yes, I think it might possibly frighten Miss Murray."

Helen raised her eyes to his, but said nothing.

"Oh, by Jove!" murmured Lord Fulkeward, feeling his moustache as usual. "Then don't you come, Miss Murray. We'll tell you all about it afterwards."

"I have no curiosity on the subject," she said a trifle coldly. "Denzil, you will find me in the drawing-room. I have a letter to write home."

With a slight salute she left them, Gervase watching the disappearance of her graceful figure with a tinge of melancholy regret in his eyes.

"It is evident Mademoiselle Helen does not like the Princess Ziska," he observed.

"Oh, well, as to that," said Fulkeward hastily, "you know you can't expect women to lose their heads about her as men do. Beside, there's something rather strange in the Princess's manner and appearance, and perhaps Miss Murray doesn't take to her any more than I do."

"Oh, then you are not one of her lovers?" queried Dr. Dean smiling.

"No; are you?"

"I? Good heavens, my dear young sir, I was never in love with a woman in my life! That is, not what You would call in love. At the age of sixteen I wrote verses to a mature young damsel of forty,—a woman with a remarkably fine figure and plenty of it; she rejected my advances with scorn, and I have never loved since!"

They all laughed,—even Denzil Murray's sullen features cleared for the moment into the brightness of a smile.

"Where did you paint the Princess's picture?" inquired Ross Courtney suddenly.

"In her own house," replied Gervase. "But we were not alone, for the fascinating fair one had some twenty or more armed servants within call." There was a movement of surprise among his listeners, and he went on: "Yes; Madame is very well protected, I assure you,—as much so as if she were the first favorite in a harem. Come now, and see my sketch."

He led the way to a private sitting-room which he had secured for himself in the hotel at almost fabulous terms. It was a small apartment, but it had the advantage of a long French window which opened out into the garden. Here, on an easel, was a canvas with its back turned towards the spectator.

"Sit down," said Gervase abruptly addressing his guests, "and be prepared for a curiosity unlike anything you have ever seen before!" He paused a moment, looking steadily at Dr. Dean. "Perhaps, Doctor, as you are interested in psychic phenomena, you may be able to explain how I got such a face on my canvas, for I cannot explain it to myself."

He slowly turned the canvas round, and, scarcely heeding the exclamation of amazement that broke simultaneously from all the men present, stared at it himself, fascinated by a singular magnetism more potent than either horror or fear.

IX

What a strange and awful face it was!—what a thing of distorted passion and pain! What an agony was expressed in every line of the features!—agony in which the traces of a divine beauty lingered only to render the whole countenance more repellent and terrific! A kind of sentient solemnity, mingled with wrath and terror, glared from the painted eyes,—the lips, slightly parted in a cruel upward curve, seemed about to utter a shriek of menace,—the hair, drooping in black, thick clusters low on the brow, looked wet as with the dews of the rigor mortis,—and to add to the mysterious horror of the whole conception, the distinct outline of a death's-head was seen plainly through the rose-brown flesh-tints. There was no real resemblance in this horrible picture to the radiant and glowing loveliness of the Princess Ziska, yet, at the same time, there was sufficient dim likeness to make an imaginative person think it might be possible for her to assume that appearance in death. Several minutes passed in utter silence,—then Lord Fulkeward suddenly rose.

"I'm going!" he said. "It's a beastly thing; it makes me sick!"

"Grand merci!" said Gervase with a forced smile.

"I really can't help it," declared the young man, turning his back to the picture. "If I am rude, you must excuse it. I'm not very strong—my mother will tell you I get put out very easily,—and I shall dream of this horrid face all night if I don't give it a wide berth."

And, without any further remark he stepped out through the open window into the garden, and walked off. Gervase made no comment on his departure; he turned his eyes towards Dr. Dean who, with spectacles on nose, was staring hard at the picture with every sign of the deepest interest.

"Well, Doctor," he said, "you see it is not at all like the Princess."

"Oh, yes it is!" returned the Doctor placidly. "If you could imagine the Princess's face in torture, it would be like her. It is the kind of expression she might wear if she suddenly met with a violent end."

"But why should I paint her so?" demanded Gervase. "She was perfectly tranquil; and her attitude was most picturesquely composed. I sketched her as I thought I saw her,—how did this tortured head come on my canvas?"

The Doctor scratched his chin thoughtfully. It was certainly a problem. He stared hard at Gervase, as though searching for the clue to the mystery in the handsome artist's own face. Then he turned to Denzil Murray, who had not stirred or spoken.

"What do you think of it, eh, Denzil?" he asked.

The young man started as from a dream.

"I don't know what to think of it."

"And you?" said the Doctor, addressing Ross Courtney.

"I? Oh, I am of the same opinion as Fulkeward,—I think it is a horrible thing. And the curious part of the matter is that it is like the Princess Ziska, and yet totally unlike. Upon my word, you know, it is a very unpleasant picture."

Dr. Dean got up and paced the room two or three times, his brows knitted in a heavy frown. Suddenly he stopped in front of Gervase.

"Tell me," he said, "have you any recollection of ever having met the Princess Ziska before?"

Gervase looked puzzled, then answered slowly:

"No, I have no actual recollection of the kind. At the same time, I admit to you that there is something about her which has always struck me as being familiar. The tone of her voice and the peculiar cadence of her laughter particularly affect me in this way. Last night when I was dancing with her, I wondered whether I had ever come across her as a model in one of the studios in Paris or Rome."

The Doctor listened to him attentively, watching him narrowly the while. But he shook his head incredulously at the idea of the Princess ever having posed as a model.

"No, no, that won't do!" he said. "I do not believe she was ever in the model business. Think again. You are now a man in the prime of life, Monsieur Gervase, but look back to your early youth,—the period when young men do wild, reckless, and often wicked things,—did you ever in that thoughtless time break a woman's heart?"

Gervase flushed, and shrugged his shoulders.

"Pardieu! I may have done! Who can tell? But if I did, what would that have to do with this?" and he tapped the picture impatiently.

The Doctor sat down and smacked his lips with a peculiar air of enjoyment.

"It would have a great deal to do with it," he answered, "that is, psychologically speaking. I have known of such cases. We will argue the point out systematically thus:—Suppose that you, in your boyhood, had wronged some woman, and suppose that woman had died. You might imagine you had got rid of that woman. But if her love was very strong and her sense of outrage very bitter, I must tell you that you have not got rid of her by any means, moreover, you never will get rid of her. And why? Because her Soul, like all Souls, is imperishable. Now, putting it as a mere supposition, and for the sake of the argument, that you feel a certain admiration for the Princess Ziska, an admiration which might possibly deepen into something more than platonic, . . ."—here Denzil Murray looked up, his eyes glowing with an angry pain as he fixed them on Gervase,—"why then the Soul of the other woman you once wronged might come between you and the face of the new attraction and cause you to unconsciously paint the tortured look of the injured and unforgiving Spirit on the countenance of the lovely fascinator whose charms are just beginning to ensnare you. I repeat, I have known of such cases." And, unheeding the amazed and incredulous looks of his listeners, the little Doctor folded both his short arms across his chest, and hugged himself in the exquisite delight of his own strange theories." The fact is," he continued," you cannot get rid of ghosts! They are all about us—everywhere! Sometimes they take forms, sometimes they are content to remain invisible. But they never fail to make their presence felt. Often during the performance of some great piece of music they drift between the air and the melody, making the sounds wilder and more haunting, and freezing the blood of the listener with a vague agony and chill. Sometimes they come between us and our friends, mysteriously forbidding any further exchange of civilities or sympathies, and occasionally they meet us alone and walk and talk with us invisibly. Generally they mean well, but sometimes they mean ill. And the only explanation I can offer you, Monsieur Gervase, as to the present picture problem is that a ghost must have come between you and your canvas!"

Gervase laughed loudly.

"My good friend, you are an adept in the art of pleading the impossible! You must excuse me; I am a sceptic; and I hope I am also in possession of my sober reason,—therefore, you can hardly wonder at my entirely refusing to accept such preposterous theories as those you appear to believe in."

Dr. Dean gave him a civil little bow.

"I do not ask you to accept them, my dear sir! I state my facts, and you can take them or leave them, just as you please. You yourself can offer no explanation of the singular way in which this picture has been produced; I offer one which is perfectly tenable with the discoveries of psychic science,—and you dismiss it as preposterous. That being the case, I should recommend you to cut up this canvas and try your hand again on the same subject."

"Of course, I shall try again," retorted Gervase. "But I do not think I shall destroy this first sketch. It is a curiosity in its way; and it has a peculiar fascination for me. Do you notice how thoroughly Egyptian the features are? They are the very contour of some of the faces on the recently-discovered frescoes."

"Oh, I noticed that at once," said the Doctor; "but that is not remarkable, seeing that you yourself are quite of an Egyptian type, though a Frenchman,—so much so, in fact, that many people in this hotel have commented on it."

Gervase said nothing, but slowly turned the canvas round with its face to the wall.

"You have seen enough of it, I suppose?" he inquired of Denzil Murray.

"More than enough!"

Gervase smiled.

"It ought to disenchant you," he said in a lower tone.

"But it is a libel on her beauty,—it is not in the least like her," returned Murray coldly.

"Not in the very least? Are you sure? My dear Denzil, you know as well as I do that there Is a likeness, combined with a dreadful unlikeness; and it is that which troubles both of us. I assure you, my good boy, I am as sorry for you as I am for myself,—for I feel that this woman will be the death of one or both of us!"

Denzil made no reply, and presently they all strolled out in the garden and lit their cigars and cigarettes, with the exception of Dr. Dean who never smoked and never drank anything stronger than water.

"I am going to get up a party for the Nile," he said as he turned his sharp, ferret-like eyes upwards to the clear heavens; "and I shall take the Princess into my confidence. In fact, I have written to her about it to-day. I hear she has a magnificent electric dahabeah, and if she will let us charter it. . ."

"She won't," said Denzil hastily, "unless she goes with it herself."

"You seem to know a great deal about her," observed Dr. Dean indulgently, "and why should she not go herself? She is evidently well instructed in the ancient history of Egypt, and, as she reads the hieroglyphs, she will be a delightful guide and a most valuable assistant to me in my researches."

"What researches are you engaged upon now?" inquired Courtney.

"I am hunting down a man called Araxes," answered the Doctor. "He lived, so far as I can make out, some four or five thousand years ago, more or less; and I want to find out what he did and how he died, and when I know how he died, then I mean to discover where he is buried. If possible, I shall excavate him. I also want to find the remains of Ziska-Charmazel, the lady impersonated by our charming friend the Princess last night,—the dancer, who, it appears from a recently-discovered fresco, occupied most of her time in dancing before this same Araxes and making herself generally agreeable to him."

"What an odd fancy!" exclaimed Denzil. "How can a man and woman dead five thousand years ago be of any interest to you?"

"What interest has Rameses?" demanded the Doctor politely, "or any of the Ptolemies? Araxes, like Rameses, may lead to fresh discoveries in Egypt, for all we know. One name is as good as another,—and each odoriferous mummy has its own mystery."

They all came just then to a pause in their walk, Gervase stopping to light a fresh cigarette. The rays of the rising moon fell upon him as he stood, a tall and stately figure, against a background of palms, and shone on his dark features with a touch of grayish-green luminance that gave him for the moment an almost spectral appearance. Dr. Dean glanced at him with a smile.

"What a figure of an Egyptian, is he not!" he said to Courtney and Denzil Murray. "Look at him! What height and symmetry! What a world of ferocity in those black, slumbrous eyes! Yes, Monsieur Gervase, I am talking about you. I am admiring you!"

"Trop d'honneur!" murmured Gervase, carefully shielding with one hand the match with which he was kindling his cigarette.

"Yes," continued the Doctor, "I am admiring you. Being a little man myself, I naturally like tall men, and as an investigator of psychic forms I am immensely interested when I see a finely-made body in which the soul lies torpid. That is why you unconsciously compose for me a wonderful subject of study. I wonder now, how long this torpidity in the psychic germ has lasted in you? It commenced, of course, originally in protoplasm; but it must have continued through various low forms and met with enormous difficulties in attaining to individual consciousness as man,—because even now it is scarcely conscious."

Gervase laughed.

"Why, that beginning of the soul in protoplasm is part of a creed which the Princess Ziska was trying to teach me to-day," he said lightly. "It's all no use. I don't believe in the soul; if I did, I should be a miserable man."

"Why?" asked Murray.

"Why? Because, my dear fellow, I should be rather afraid of my future. I should not like to live again; I might have to remember certain incidents which I would rather forget. There is your charming sister, Mademoiselle Helen! I must go and talk to her,—her conversation always does me good; and after that picture which I have been unfortunate enough to produce, her presence will be as soothing as the freshness of morning after an unpleasant nightmare."

He moved away; Denzil Murray with Courtney followed him. Dr. Dean remained behind, and presently sitting down in a retired corner of the garden alone, he took out a small pocket-book and stylographic pen and occupied himself for more than half an hour in busily writing till he had covered two or three pages with his small, neat caligraphy.

"It is the most interesting problem I ever had the chance of studying!" he murmured half aloud when he had finished, "Of course, if my researches into the psychic spheres of action are worth anything, it can only be one case out of thousands. Thousands? Aye, perhaps millions! Great heavens! Among what terrific unseen forces we live! And in exact proportion to every man's arrogant denial of the 'Divinity that shapes our ends, so will be measured out to him the revelation of the invisible. Strange that the human race has never entirely realized as yet the depth of meaning in the words describing hell:' Where the worm dieth not, and where the flame is never quenched. The 'worm' is Retribution, the 'flame' is the immortal Spirit,—and the two are forever striving to escape from the other. Horrible! And yet there are men who believe in neither one thing nor the other, and reject the Redemption that does away with both! God forgive us all our sins,—and especially the sins of pride and presumption!"

And with a shade of profound melancholy on his features, the little Doctor put by his note-book, and, avoiding all the hotel loungers on the terrace and elsewhere, retired to his own room and went to bed.

X

The next day when Armand Gervase went to call on the Princess Ziska he was refused admittance. The Nubian attendant who kept watch and ward at her gates, hearing the door-bell ring, contented himself with thrusting his ugly head through an open upper window and shouting—

"Madame est sortie!"

"Ou donc?" called Gervase in answer.

"A la campagne—le desert—les pyramides!" returned the Nubian, at the same time banging the lattice to in order to prevent the possibility of any further conversation. And Gervase, standing in the street irresolutely for a moment, fancied he heard a peal of malicious laughter in the distance.

"Beast!" he muttered, "I must try him with a money bribe next time I get hold of him. I wonder what I shall do with myself now?—haunted and brain-ridden as I am by this woman and her picture?"

The hot sun glared in his eyes and made them ache,—the rough stones of the narrow street were scorching to his feet. He began to move slowly away with a curious faint sensation of giddiness and sickness upon him, when the sound of music floating from the direction of the Princess Ziska's palace brought him to a sudden standstill. It was a strange, wild melody, played on some instrument with seemingly muffled strings. A voice with a deep, throbbing thrill of sweetness in it began to sing:

> *Oh, for the passionless peace of the Lotus-Lily!*
> *It floats in a waking dream on the waters chilly,*
> *With its leaves unfurled*
> *To the wondering world,*
> *Knowing naught of the sorrow and restless pain*
> *That burns and tortures the human brain;*
> *Oh, for the passionless peace of the Lotus-Lily!*
>
> *Oh, for the pure cold heart of the Lotus-Lily!*
> *Bared to the moon on the waters dark and chilly.*
> *A star above*
> *Is its only love,*

And one brief sigh of its scented breath
Is all it will ever know of Death;
Oh, for the pure cold heart of the Lotus-Lily!

When the song ceased, Gervase raised his eyes from the ground on which he had fixed them in a kind of brooding stupor, and stared at the burning blue of the sky as vaguely and wildly as a sick man in the delirium of fever.

"God! What ails me!" he muttered, supporting himself with one hand against the black and crumbling wall near which he stood. "Why should that melody steal away my strength and make me think of things with which I have surely no connection! What tricks my imagination plays me in this city of the Orient—I might as well be hypnotized! What have I to do with dreams of war and triumph and rapine and murder, and what is the name of Ziska-Charmazel to me?"

He shook himself with the action of a fine brute that has been stung by some teasing insect, and, mastering his emotions by an effort, walked away. But he was so absorbed in strange thoughts, that he stumbled up against Denzil Murray in a side street on the way to the Gezireh Palace Hotel without seeing him, and would have passed him altogether had not Denzil somewhat fiercely said:

"Stop!"

Gervase looked at him bewilderedly.

"Why, Denzil, is it you? My dear fellow, forgive me my brusquerie! I believe I have got a stroke of the sun, or something of the sort; I assure you I hardly know what I am doing or where I am going!"

"I believe it!" said Denzil, hoarsely. "You are as mad as I am—for love!"

Gervase smiled; a slight incredulous smile.

"You think so? I am not sure! If love makes a man as thoroughly unstrung and nervous as I am to-day, then love is a very bad illness."

"It is the worst illness in the world," said Denzil, speaking hurriedly and wildly. "The most cruel and torturing! And there is no cure for it save death. My God, Gervase! You were my friend but yesterday! I never should have thought it possible to hate you!"

"Yet you do hate me?" queried Gervase, still smiling a little.

"Hate you? I could kill you! You have been with HER!"

Quietly Gervase took his arm.

"My good Denzil, you are mistaken! I confess to you frankly I should have been with HER—you mean the Princess Ziska, of course—had it been possible. But she has fled the city for the moment—at least, according to the corpse-like Nubian who acts as porter."

"He lies!" exclaimed Denzil, hotly. "I saw her this morning."

"I hope you improved your opportunity," said Gervase, imperturbably. "Anyway, at the present moment she is not visible."

A silence fell between them for some minutes; then Denzil spoke again.

"Gervase, it is no use, I cannot stand this sort of thing. We must have it out. What does it all mean?"

"It is difficult to explain, my dear boy," answered Gervase, half seriously, half mockingly. "It means, I presume, that we are both in love with the same woman, and that we both intend to try our chances with her. But, as I told you the other night, I do not see why we should quarrel about it. Your intentions towards the Princess are honorable—mine are dishonorable, and I shall make no secret of them. If you win her, I shall. . ."

He paused, and there was a sudden look in his eyes which gave them a sombre darkness, darker than their own natural color.

"You shall—what?" asked Denzil.

"Do something desperate," replied Gervase. "What the something will be depends on the humor of the moment. A tiger balked of his prey is not an agreeable beast; a strong man deprived of the woman he passionately desires is a little less agreeable even than the tiger. But let us adopt the policy of laissez-faire. Nothing is decided; the fair one cares for neither of us; let us be friends until she makes her choice."

"We cannot be friends," said Denzil, sternly.

"Good! Let us be foes then, but courteous, even in our quarrel, dear boy. If we must kill each other, let us do it civilly. To fly at each other's throats would be purely barbaric. We owe a certain duty to civilization; things have progressed since the days of Araxes."

Denzil stared at him gloomily.

"Araxes is Dr. Dean's fad," he said. "I don't know anything about Egyptian mummies, and don't want to know. My matter is with the present, and not with the past."

They had reached the hotel by this time, and turned into the gardens side by side.

"You understand?" repeated Denzil. "We cannot be friends!"

Gervase gave him a profoundly courteous salute, and the two separated.

Later on in the afternoon, about an hour before dinner-time, Gervase, strolling on the terrace of the hotel alone, saw Helen Murray seated at a little distance under some trees, with a book in her hand which she was not reading. There were tears in her eyes, but as he approached her she furtively dashed them away and greeted him with a poor attempt at a smile.

"You have a moment to spare me?" he asked, sitting down beside her.

She bent her head in acquiescence.

"I am a very unhappy man, Mademoiselle Helen," he began, looking at her with a certain compassionate tenderness as he spoke. "I want your sympathy, but I know I do not deserve it."

Helen remained silent. A faint flush crimsoned her cheeks, but her eyes were veiled under the long lashes—she thought he could not see them.

"You remember," he went on, "our pleasant times in Scotland? Ah, it is a restful place, your Highland home, with the beautiful purple hills rolling away in the distance, and the glorious moors covered with fragrant heather, and the gurgling of the river that runs between birch and fir and willow, making music all day long for those who have the ears to listen, and the hearts to understand the pretty love tune it sings! You know Frenchmen always have more or less sympathy with the Scotch—some old association, perhaps, with the romantic times of Mary Queen of Scots, when the light and changeful fancies of Chastelard and his brother poets and lutists made havoc in the hearts of many a Highland maiden. What is that bright drop on your hand, Helen?—are you crying?" He waited a moment, and his voice was softer and more tremulous. "Dear girl, I am not worthy of tears. I am not good enough for you."

He gave her time to recover her momentary emotion and then went on, still softly and tenderly:

"Listen, Helen. I want you to believe me and forgive me, if you can. I know—I remember those moonlight evenings in Scotland—holy and happy evenings, as sweet as flower-scented pages in a young girl's missal; yes, and I did not mean to play with you, Helen, or wound your gentle heart. I almost loved you!" He spoke the words passionately, and for a moment she raised her eyes and looked at him in something of fear as well as sorrow. "'Yes,' I said to my self, 'this woman, so true and pure and fair, is a bride for a king; and if I can win her—if!' Ah, there my musings stopped. But I came to Egypt chiefly to meet you again, knowing that you and your brother were in Cairo. How was I to know, how was I to guess that this horrible thing would happen?"

Helen gazed at him wonderingly.

"What horrible thing?" she asked, falteringly, the rich color coming and going on her face, and her heart beating violently as she put the question.

His eyes flashed.

"This," he answered. "The close and pernicious enthralment of a woman I never met till the night before last; a woman whose face haunts me; a woman who drags me to her side with the force of a magnet, there to grovel like a brain-sick fool and plead with her for a love which I already know is poison to my soul! Helen, Helen! You do not understand—you will never understand! Here, in the very air I breathe, I fancy I can trace the perfume she shakes from her garments as she moves; something indescribably fascinating yet terrible attracts me to her; it is an evil attraction, I know, but I cannot resist it. There is something wicked in every man's nature; I am conscious enough that there is something detestably wicked in mine, and I have not sufficient goodness to overbalance it. And this woman,—this silent, gliding, glittering-eyed creature that has suddenly taken possession of my fancy—she overcomes me in spite of myself; she makes havoc of all the good intentions of my life. I admit it—I confess it!"

"You are speaking of the Princess Ziska?" asked Helen, tremblingly.

"Of whom else should I speak?" he responded, dreamily. "There is no one like her; probably there never was anyone like her, except, perhaps, Ziska-Charmazel!"

As the name passed his lips, he sprang hastily up and stood amazed, as though some sudden voice had called him. Helen Murray looked at him in alarm.

"Oh, what is it?" she exclaimed.

He forced a laugh.

"Nothing—nothing—but a madness! I suppose it is all a part of my strange malady. Your brother is stricken with the same fever. Surely you know that?"

"Indeed I do know it," Helen answered, "to my sorrow!"

He regarded her intently. Her face in its pure outline and quiet sadness of expression touched him more than he cared to own even to himself.

"My dear Helen," he said, with an effort at composure, "I have been talking wildly; you must forgive me! Don't think about me at all; I am not worth it! Denzil has taken it into his head to quarrel with me on account of the Princess Ziska, but I assure you I will not quarrel with him. He is infatuated, and so am I. The best thing for all of us to do would be to leave Egypt instantly; I feel that instinctively, only we cannot do it. Something holds us here. You will never persuade Denzil to go, and I—I cannot persuade myself to go. There is a clinging sweetness in the air for me; and there are vague suggestions, memories, dreams, histories—wonderful things which hold me spell-bound! I wish I could analyze them, recognize them, or understand them. But I cannot, and there, perhaps, is their secret charm. Only one thing grieves me, and that is, that I have, perhaps, unwittingly, in some thoughtless way, given you pain; is it so, Helen?"

She rose quickly, and with a quiet dignity held out her hand.

"No, Monsieur Gervase," she said, "it is not so. I am not one of those women who take every little idle word said by men in jest au grand serieux! You have always been a kind and courteous friend, and if you ever fancied you had a warmer feeling for me, as you say, I am sure you were mistaken. We often delude ourselves in these matters. I wish, for your sake, I could think the Princess Ziska worthy of the love she so readily inspires. But,—I cannot! My brother's infatuation for her is to me terrible. I feel it will break his heart,—and mine!" A little half sob caught her breath and interrupted her; she paused, but presently went on with an effort at calmness: "You talk of our leaving Egypt; how I wish that were possible! But I spoke to Denzil about it on the night of the ball, and he was furious with me for the mere suggestion. It seems like an evil fate."

"It Is an evil fate," said Gervase gloomily. "Enfin, my dear Helen, we cannot escape from it,—at least, *I* cannot. But I never was intended for good things, not even for a lasting love. A lasting love I feel would bore me. You look amazed; you believe in lasting love? So do many sweet women. But do you know what symbol I, as an artist, would employ were I asked to give my idea of Love on my canvas?"

Helen smiled sadly and shook her head.

"I would paint a glowing flame," said Gervase dreamily. "A flame leaping up from the pit of hell to the height of heaven, springing in darkness, lost in light; and flying into the centre of that flame should be a white moth—a blind, soft, mad thing with beating, tremulous wings,—that should be Love! Whirled into the very heart of the ravening fire,—crushed, shrivelled out of existence in one wild, rushing rapture—that is what Love must be to me! One cannot prolong passion over fifty years, more or less, of commonplace routine, as marriage would have us do. The very notion is absurd. Love is like a choice wine of exquisite bouquet and intoxicating flavor; it is the most maddening draught in the world, but you cannot drink it every day. No, my dear Helen; I am not made for a quiet life,—nor for a long one, I fancy."

His voice unconsciously sank into a melancholy tone, and for one moment Helen's composure nearly gave way. She loved him as true women love, with that sublime self-sacrifice which only desires the happiness of the thing beloved; yet a kind of insensate rage stirred for once in her gentle soul to think that the mere sight of a strange woman with dark eyes,—a woman whom no one knew anything about, and who was by some people deemed a mere adventuress,—should have so overwhelmed this man whose genius she had deemed superior to fleeting impressions. Controlling the tears that rose to her eyes and threatened to fall, she said gently,

"Good-bye, Monsieur Gervase!"

He started as from a reverie.

"Good-bye, Helen! Some day you will think kindly of me again?"

"I think kindly of you now," she answered tremulously; then, not trusting herself to say any more, she turned swiftly and left him.

"The flame and the moth!" he mused, watching her slight figure till it had disappeared. "Yes, it is the only fitting symbol. Love must be always so. Sudden, impetuous, ungovernable, and then—the end! To stretch out the divine passion over life-long breakfasts and dinners! It would be intolerable to me. Lord Fulkeward could do that sort of thing; his chest is narrow, and his sentiments are as limited as his chest. He would duly kiss his wife every morning and evening, and he would not analyze the fact that no special thrill of joy stirred in him at the action. What should he do with thrills of joy—this poor Fulkeward? And yet it is likely he will marry Helen. Or will it be the Courtney animal,—the type of man whose one idea is 'to arise, kill, and eat?' "Ah, well!" and he sighed. "She is not for me, this maiden grace of womanhood. If I married her, I should make her miserable. I am made for passion, not for peace."

He started as he heard a step behind him, and turning, saw Dr. Dean. The worthy little savant looked worried and preoccupied.

"I have had a letter from the Princess Ziska," he said, without any preliminary. "She has gone to secures rooms at the Mena House Hotel, which is situated close to the Pyramids. She regrets she cannot enter into the idea of taking a trip up the Nile. She has no time, she says, as she is soon leaving Cairo. But she suggests that we should make up a party for the Mena House while she is staying there, as she can, so she tells me, make the Pyramids much more interesting for us by her intimate knowledge of them. Now, to me this is a very tempting offer, but I should not care to go alone."

"The Murrays will go, I am sure," murmured Gervase lazily. "At any rate, Denzil will."

The Doctor looked at him narrowly.

"If Denzil goes, so will you go," he said. "Thus there are two already booked for company. And I fancy the Fulkewards might like the idea."

"The Princess is leaving Cairo?" queried Gervase presently, as though it were an after thought.

"So she informs me in her letter. The party which is to come off on Wednesday night is her last reception."

Gervase was silent a moment. Then he said:

"Have you told Denzil?"

"Not yet."

"Better do so then," and Gervase glanced up at the sky, now glowing red with a fiery sunset. "He wants to propose, you know."

"Good God!" cried the Doctor, sharply, "If he proposes to that woman. . ."

"Why should he not?" demanded Gervase. "Is she not as ripe for love and fit for marriage as any other of her sex?"

"Her sex!" echoed the Doctor grimly. "Her sex!—There!—for heaven's sake don't talk to me!—leave me alone! The Princess Ziska is like no woman living; she has none of the sentiments of a woman,— and the notion of Denzil's being such a fool as to think of proposing to her—Oh, leave me alone, I tell you! Let me worry this out!"

And clapping his hat well down over his eyes, he began to walk away in a strange condition of excitement, which he evidently had some difficulty in suppressing. Suddenly, however, he turned, came back and tapped Gervase smartly on the chest.

"You are the man for the Princess," he said impressively. "There is a madness in you which you call love for her; you are her fitting mate, not that poor boy, Denzil Murray. In certain men and women spirit leaps to spirit,—note responds to note—and if all the world were to interpose its trumpery bulk, nothing could prevent such tumultuous forces rushing together. Follow your destiny, Monsieur Gervase, but do not ruin another man's life on the way. Follow your destiny,—complete it,—you are bound to do so,—but in the havoc and wildness to come, for God's sake, let the innocent go free!"

He spoke with extraordinary solemnity, and Gervase stared at him in utter bewilderment and perplexity, not understanding in the least what he meant. But before he could interpose a word or ask a question, Dr. Dean had gone.

The next two or three days passed without any incident of interest occurring to move the languid calm and excite the fleeting interest of the fashionable English and European visitors who were congregated at the Gezireh Palace Hotel. The anxious flirtations of Dolly and Muriel Chetwynd Lyle afforded subjects of mirth to the profane,—the wonderfully youthful toilettes of Lady Fulkeward provided several keynotes from which to strike frivolous conversation,—and when the great painter, Armand Gervase, actually made a sketch of her ladyship for his own amusement, and made her look about sixteen, and girlish at that, his popularity knew no bounds. Everyone wanted to give him a commission, particularly the elderly fair, and he could have made a fortune had he chosen, after the example set him by the English academicians, by painting the portraits of ugly nobodies who were ready to pay any price to be turned out as handsome somebodies. But he was too restless and ill at ease to apply himself steadily to work,—the glowing skies of Egypt, the picturesque groups of natives to be seen at every turn,—the curious corners of old Cairo—these made no impression upon his mind at all, and when he was alone, he passed whole half hours staring at the strange picture he had made of the Princess Ziska, wherein the face of death seemed confronting him through a mask of life. And he welcomed with a strong sense of relief and expectation the long-looked-for evening of the Princess's "reception," to which many of the visitors in Cairo had been invited since a fortnight, and which those persons who always profess to be "in the know," even if they are wallowing in ignorance, declared would surpass any entertainment ever given during the Cairene season.

The night came at last. It was exceedingly sultry, but bright and clear, and the moon shone with effective brilliance on the gayly-attired groups of people that between nine and ten o'clock began to throng the narrow street in which the carved tomb-like portal of the Princess Ziska's residence was the most conspicuous object. Lady Chetwynd Lyle, remarkable for bad taste in her dress and the disposal of her diamonds, stared in haughty amazement at the Nubian, who saluted her and her daughters with the grin peculiar to his uninviting cast of countenance, and swept into the courtyard attended by her husband with an air as though she imagined her presence gave the necessary flavor of "good style" to the proceedings. She was followed by Lady Fulkeward, innocently clad in white and wearing a knot of lilies on her prettily-enamelled left shoulder, Lord Fulkeward, Denzil Murray and his sister. Helen also wore white, but though she was in the twenties and Lady Fulkeward was in the sixties, the girl had so much sadness in her face and so much tragedy in her soft eyes that she looked, if anything, older than the old woman. Gervase and Dr. Dean arrived together, and found themselves in a brilliant, crushing crowd of people, all of different nationalities and all manifesting a good deal of impatience because they were delayed a few minutes in an open court, where a couple of stone lions with wings were the only spectators of their costumes.

"Most singular behavior!" said Lady Chetwynd Lyle, snorting and sniffing, "to keep us waiting outside like this! The Princess has no idea of European manners!"

As she spoke, a sudden blaze of light flamed on the scene, and twenty tall Egyptian servants in white, with red turbans, carrying lighted torches and marching two by two crossed the court, and by mute yet stately gestures invited the company to follow. And the company did follow in haste, with scramble and rudeness, as is the way of "European manners" nowadays; and presently, having been relieved of their cloaks and wrappings, stood startled and confounded in a huge hall richly adorned with silk and cloth of gold hangings, where, between two bronze sphinxes, the Princess Ziska, attired wonderfully in a dim, pale rose color, with flecks of jewels flashing from her draperies here and there, waited to receive her guests. Like a queen she stood,—behind her towered a giant palm, and at her feet were strewn roses and lotus-lilies. On either side of her, seated on the ground, were young girls gorgeously clad and veiled to the eyes in the Egyptian fashion, and as the staring, heated and impetuous swarm of "travelling" English and Americans came face to face with her in her marvellous beauty, they were for the moment stricken spellbound, and could scarcely summon up the necessary assurance to advance and take the hand she outstretched to them in welcome. She appeared not to see the general embarrassment, and greeted all who approached her with courteous ease and composure, speaking the few words which every graceful hostess deems adequate before "passing on" her visitors. And presently music began,—music wild and fantastic, of a character unknown to modern fashionable ears, yet strangely familiar to Armand Gervase, who started at the first sound of it, and seemed enthralled.

"That is not an ordinary orchestra," said Dr. Dean in his ear. "The instruments are ancient, and the form of melody is barbaric."

Gervase answered nothing, for the Princess Ziska just then approached them.

"Come into the Red Saloon," she said. "I am persuading my guests to pass on there. I have an old bas-relief on the walls which I would like you to see,—you, especially, Dr. Dean!—for you are so learned in antiquities. I hear you are trying to discover traces of Araxes?"

"I am," replied the Doctor. "You interested me very much in his history."

"He was a great man," said the Princess, slowly piloting them as she spoke, without hurry and with careful courtesy, through the serried ranks of the now freely chattering and animated company. "Much greater than any of your modern heroes. But he had two faults; faults which frequently accompany the plentitude of power,—cruelty and selfishness. He betrayed and murdered the only woman that ever loved him, Ziska-Charmazel."

"Murdered her!" exclaimed Dr. Dean. "How?"

"Oh, it is only a legend!" and the Princess smiled, turning her dark eyes with a bewitching languor on Gervase, who, for some reason or other which he could not explain, felt as if he were walking in a dream on the edge of a deep chasm of nothingness, into which he must presently sink to utter destruction. "All these old histories happened so long ago that they are nothing but myths now to the present generation."

"Time does not rob any incident of its interest to me," said Dr. Dean. "Ages hence Queen Victoria will be as much a doubtful potentate as King Lud. To the wise student of things there is no time and no distance. All history from the very beginning is like a wonderful chain in which no link is ever really broken, and in which every part fits closely to the other part,—though why the chain should exist at all is a mystery we cannot solve. Yet I am quite certain that even our late friend Araxes has his connection with the present, if only for the reason that he lived in the past."

"How do you argue out that theory!" asked Gervase with sudden interest.

"How do you argue it? The question is, how can you argue at all about anything that is so plain and demonstrated a fact? The doctrine of evolution proves it. Everything that we were once has its part in us now. Suppose, if you like, that we were originally no more than shells on the shore,—some remnant of the nature of the shell must be in us at this moment. Nothing is lost,—nothing is wasted,—not even a thought. I carry my theories very far," pursued the Doctor, looking keenly from one to the other of his silent companions as they walked beside him through a long corridor towards the Red Saloon, which could be seen, brilliantly lit up and thronged with people. "Very far indeed, especially in regard to matters of love. I maintain that if it is decreed that the soul of a man and the soul of a woman must meet,—must rush together,—not all the forces of the universe can hinder them; aye, even if they were, for some conventional cause or circumstance themselves reluctant to consummate their destiny, it would nevertheless, despite them, be consummated. For mark you,—in some form or other they have rushed together before! Whether as flames in the air, or twining leaves on a tree, or flowers in a field, they have felt the sweetness and fitness of each other's being in former lives,—and the craving sense of that sweetness and fitness can never be done away with,—never! Not as long as this present universe lasts! It is a terrible thing," continued the Doctor in a lower tone, "a terrible fatality,—the desire of love. In some cases it is a curse; in others, a divine and priceless blessing. The results depend entirely on the temperaments of the human creatures possessed by its fever. When it kindles, rises and burns towards Heaven in a steady flame of ever-brightening purity and faith, then it makes marriage the most perfect union on earth,—the sweetest and most blessed companionship; but when it is a mere gust of fire, bright and fierce as the sudden leaping light of a volcano, then it withers everything at a touch,—faith, honor, truth,—and dies into dull ashes in which no spark remains to warm or inspire man's higher nature. Better death than such a love,—for it works misery on earth; but who can tell what horrors it may not create Hereafter!"

The Princess looked at him with a strange, weird gleam in her dark eyes.

"You are right," she said. "It is just the Hereafter that men never think of. I am glad you, at least, acknowledge the truth of the life beyond death."

"I am bound to acknowledge it," returned the Doctor; "inasmuch as I know it exists."

Gervase glanced at him with a smile, in which there was something of contempt.

"You are very much behind the age, Doctor," he remarked lightly.

"Very much behind indeed," agreed Dr. Dean composedly. "The age rushes on too rapidly for me, and gives no time to the consideration of things by the way. I stop,—I take breathing space in which to think; life without thought is madness, and I desire to have no part in a mad age."

At that moment they entered the Red Saloon, a stately apartment, which was entirely modelled after the most ancient forms of Egyptian architecture. The centre of the vast room was quite clear of furniture, so that the Princess Ziska's guests went wandering up and down, to and fro, entirely at their ease, without crush or inconvenience, and congregated in corners for conversation; though if they chose they could recline on low divans and gorgeously-cushioned benches ranged against the walls and sheltered by tall palms and flowering exotics. The music was heard to better advantage here than in the hall where the company had first been received; and as the Princess moved to a seat under the pale green frondage of a huge tropical fern and bade her two companions sit beside her, sounds of the wildest, most melancholy and haunting character began to palpitate upon the air in the mournful, throbbing fashion in which a nightingale sings when its soul is burdened with love. The passionate tremor that shakes the bird's throat at mating-time seemed to shake the unseen instruments that now discoursed strange melody, and Gervase, listening dreamily, felt a curious contraction and aching at his heart and a sense of suffocation in his throat, combined with an insatiate desire to seize in his arms the mysterious Ziska, with her dark fathomless eyes and slight, yet voluptuous, form,—to drag her to his breast and crush her there, whispering:

"Mine!—mine! By all the gods of the past and present—mine! Who shall tear her from me,—who dispute my right to love her—ruin her—murder her, if I choose? She is mine!"

"The bas-relief I told you of is just above us," said the Princess then, addressing herself to the Doctor; "would you like to examine it? One of the servants shall bring you a lighted taper, and by passing it in front of the sculpture you will be able to see the design better. Ah, Mr. Murray!" and she smiled as she greeted Denzil, who just then approached. "You are in time to give us your opinion. I want Dr. Dean to see that very old piece of stone carving on the wall above us,—it will serve as a link for him in the history of Araxes."

"Indeed!" murmured Denzil, somewhat abstractedly.

The Princess glanced at his brooding face and laughed.

"You, I know, are not interested at all in old history," she went on. "The past has no attraction for you."

"No. The present is enough," he replied, with a glance of mingled hope and passion.

She smiled, and signing to one of her Egyptian attendants, bade him bring a lighted taper. He did so, and passed it slowly up and down and to the right and left of the large piece of ancient sculpture that occupied more than half the wall, while Dr. Dean stood by, spectacles on nose, to examine the carving as closely as possible. Several other people, attracted by what was going on, paused to look also, and the Princess undertook to explain the scene depicted.

"This piece of carving is of the date of the King Amenhotep or Amenophis III, of the Eighteenth Dynasty. It represents the return of the warrior Araxes, a favorite servant of the king's, after some brilliant victory. You see, there is the triumphal car in which he rides, drawn by winged horses, and behind him are the solar deities—Ra, Sikar, Tmu, and Osiris. He is supposed to be approaching his palace in triumph; the gates are thrown open to receive him, and coming out to meet him is the chief favorite of his harem, the celebrated dancer of that period—Ziska-Charmazel."

"Whom he afterwards murdered, you say?" queried Dr. Dean meditatively.

"Yes. He murdered her simply because she loved him too well and was in the way of his ambition. There was nothing astonishing in his behavior, not even if you consider it in the light of modern times. Men always murder—morally, if not physically—the women who love them too well."

"You truly think that?" asked Denzil Murray in a low tone.

"I not only truly think it, I truly know it!" she answered, with a disdainful flash of her eyes. "Of course, I speak of strong men with strong passions; they are the only kind of men women ever worship. Of course, a weak, good-natured man is different; he would probably not harm a woman for the world, or give her the least cause for pain if he could help it, but that sort of man never becomes either an adept or a master in love. Araxes was probably both. No doubt he considered he had a perfect right to slay what he had grown weary of; he thought no more than men of his type think to-day, that the taking of a life demands a life in exchange, if not in this world, then in the next."

The group of people near her were all silent, gazing with an odd fascination at the quaint and ancient-sculptured figures above them, when all at once Dr. Dean, taking the taper from the hands of the

Egyptian servant, held the flame close to the features of the warrior riding in the car of triumph, and said slowly:

"Do you not see a curious resemblance, Princess, between this Araxes and a friend of ours here present? Monsieur Armand Gervase, will you kindly step forward? Yes, that will do, turn your head slightly,—so! Yes! Now observe the outline of the features of Araxes as carven in this sculpture thousands of years ago, and compare it with the outline of the features of our celebrated friend, the greatest French artist of his day. Am I the only one who perceives the remarkable similarity of contour and expression?"

The Princess made no reply. A smile crossed her lips, but no word escaped them. Several persons, however, pressed eagerly forward to look at and comment upon what was indeed a startling likeness. The same straight, fierce brows, the same proud, firm mouth, the same almond-shaped eyes were, as it seemed, copied from the ancient entablature and repeated in flesh and blood in the features of Gervase. Even Denzil Murray, absorbed though he was in conflicting thoughts of his own, was struck by the coincidence.

"It is really very remarkable!" he said. "Allowing for the peculiar style of drawing and design common to ancient Egypt, the portrait of Araxes might pass for Gervase in Egyptian costume."

Gervase himself was silent. Some mysterious emotion held him mute, and he was only aware of a vague irritation that fretted him without any seemingly adequate cause. Dr. Dean meanwhile pursued his investigations with the lighted taper, and presently, turning round on the assembled little group of bystanders, he said:

"I have just discovered another singular thing. The face of the woman here—the dancer and favorite—is the face of our charming hostess, the Princess Ziska!"

Exclamations of wonder greeted this announcement, and everybody craned their necks to see. And then the Princess spoke, slowly and languidly.

"Yes," she murmured, "I was hoping you would perceive that. I myself noticed how very like me is the famous Ziska-Charmazel, and that is just why I dressed in her fashion for the fancy ball the other evening. It seemed to me the best thing to do, as I wanted to choose an ancient period, and then, you know, I bear half her name."

Dr. Dean looked at her keenly, and a somewhat grim smile wrinkled his lips.

"You could not have done better," he declared. "You and the dancing-girl of Araxes might be twin sisters."

He lowered the taper he held that it might more strongly illumine her face, and as the outline of her head and throat and bust was thrown into full relief, Gervase, staring at her, was again conscious of that sudden, painful emotion of familiarity which had before overwhelmed him, and he felt that in all the world he had no such intimate knowledge of any woman as he had of Ziska. He knew her! Ah!—how did he NOT know her? Every curve of that pliant form was to him the living memory of something once possessed and loved, and he pressed his hand heavily across his eyes for a moment to shut out the sight of all the exquisite voluptuous grace which shook his self-control and tempted him almost beyond man's mortal endurance.

"Are you not well, Monsieur Gervase?" said Dr. Dean, observing him closely, and handing back the lighted taper to the Egyptian servant who waited to receive it. "The portraits on this old carving have perhaps affected you unpleasantly? Yet there is really nothing of importance in such a coincidence."

"Nothing of importance, perhaps, but surely something of singularity," interrupted Denzil Murray, "especially in the resemblance between the Princess and the dancing-girl of that ancient period,—their features are positively line for line alike."

The Princess laughed.

"Yes, is it not curious?" she said, and, taking the taper from her servant, she sprang lightly on one of the benches near the wall and leaned her beautiful head on the entablature, so that her profile stood out close against that of the once reputed Ziska-Charmazel. "We are, as Dr. Dean says, twins!"

Several of the guests had now gathered together in that particular part of the room, and they all looked up at her as she stood thus, in silent and somewhat superstitious wonderment. The fascinating dancer, famed in ages past, and the lovely, living charmeresse of the present were the image of each other, and so extraordinary was the resemblance that it was almost what some folks would term "uncanny." The fair Ziska did not, however, give her acquaintances time for much meditation or surprise concerning the matter, for she soon came down from her elevation near the sculptured frieze and, extinguishing the taper she held, she said lightly:

"As Dr. Dean has remarked, there is really nothing of importance in the coincidence. Ages ago, in the time of Araxes, roses must have bloomed; and who shall say that a rose in to-day's garden is not precisely the same in size, scent and color as one that Araxes himself plucked at his palace gates? Thus, if flowers are born alike in different ages, why not women and men?"

"Very well argued, Princess," said the Doctor. "I quite agree with you. Nature is bound to repeat some of her choicest patterns, lest she should forget the art of making them."

There was now a general movement among the guests, that particular kind of movement which means irritability and restlessness, and implies that either supper must be immediately served, or else some novel entertainment be brought in to distract attention and prevent tedium. The Princess, turning to Gervase, said smilingly:

"Apropos of the dancing-girl of Araxes and the art of dancing generally, I am going to entertain the company presently by letting them see a real old dance of Thebes. If you will excuse me a moment I must just prepare them and get the rooms slightly cleared. I will return to you presently."

She glided away with her usual noiseless grace, and within a few minutes of her departure the gay crowds began to fall back against the walls and disperse themselves generally in expectant groups here and there, the Egyptian servants moving in and out and evidently informing them of the entertainment in prospect.

"Well, I shall stay here," said Dr. Dean, "underneath this remarkable stone carving of your warrior-prototype, Monsieur Gervase. You seem very much abstracted. I asked you before if you were not well; but you never answered me."

"I am perfectly well," replied Gervase, with some irritation. "The heat is rather trying, that is all. But I attach no importance to that stone frieze. One can easily imagine likenesses where there are really none."

"True!" and the Doctor smiled to himself, and said no more. Just then a wild burst of music sounded suddenly through the apartment, and he turned round in lively anticipation to watch the proceedings.

The middle of the room was now quite clear, and presently, moving with the silent grace of swans on still water, came four girls closely veiled, carrying quaintly-shaped harps and lutes. A Nubian servant followed them, and spread a gold-embroidered carpet upon the ground, whereon they all sat down and began to thrum the strings of their instruments in a muffled, dreamy manner, playing a music which had nothing of melody in it, and which yet vaguely suggested a passionate tune. This thrumming went on for some time when all at once from a side entrance in the hall a bright, apparently winged thing bounded from the outer darkness into the centre of the hall,—a woman clad in glistening cloth of gold and veiled entirely in misty folds of white, who, raising her arms gleaming with jewelled bangles high above her head, remained poised on tiptoe for a moment, as though about to fly. Her bare feet, white and dimpled, sparkled with gems and glittering anklets; her skirts as she moved showed fluttering flecks of white and pink like the leaves of May-blossoms shaken by a summer breeze; the music grew louder and wilder, and a brazen clang from unseen cymbals prepared her as it seemed for flight. She began her dance slowly, gliding mysteriously from side to side, anon turning suddenly with her head lifted, as though listening for some word of love which should recall her or command; then, bending down again, she seemed to float lazily like a creature that was dancing in a dream without conscious knowledge of her actions. The brazen cymbals clashed again, and then, with a wild, beautiful movement, like that of a hunted stag leaping the brow of a hill, the dancer sprang forward, turned, pirouetted and tossed herself round and round giddily with a marvellous and exquisite celerity, as if she were nothing but a bright circle of gold spinning in clear ether. Spontaneous applause broke forth from every part of the hall; the guests crowded forward, staring and almost breathless with amazement. Dr. Dean got up in a state of the greatest excitement, clapping his hands involuntarily; and Gervase, every nerve in his body quivering, advanced one or two steps, feeling that he must stop this bright, wild, wanton thing in her incessant whirling, or else die in the hunger of love which consumed his soul. Denzil Murray glanced at him, and, after a pause, left his side and disappeared. Suddenly, with a quick movement, the dancer loosened her golden dress and misty veil, and tossing them aside like falling leaves, she stood confessed—a marvellous, glowing vision in silvery white-no other than the Princess Ziska!

Shouts echoed from every part of the hall:

"Ziska! Ziska!"

And at the name Lady Chetwynd Lyle rose in all her majesty from the seat she had occupied till then, and in tones of virtuous indignation said to Lady Fulkeward:

"I told you the Princess was not a proper person! Now it is proved I am right! To think I should have brought Dolly and Muriel here! I shall really never forgive myself! Come, Sir Chetwynd,—let us leave this place instantly!"

And stout Sir Chetwynd, gloating on the exquisite beauty of the Princess Ziska's form as she still danced on in her snowy white attire, her lovely face alight with mirth at the surprise she had made for her guests, tried his best to look sanctimonious and signally failed in the attempt as he answered:

"Certainly! Certainly, my dear! Most improper. . . most astonishing!"

While Lady Fulkeward answered innocently:

"Is it? Do you really think so? Oh, dear! I suppose it is improper,—it must be, you know; but it is most delightful and original!"

And while the Chetwynd Lyles thus moved to depart in a cloud of outraged propriety, followed by others who likewise thought it well to pretend to be shocked at the proceeding, Gervase, dizzy, breathless, and torn by such conflicting passions as he could never express, was in a condition more mad than sane.

"My God!" he muttered under his breath. "This—this is love! This is the beginning and end of life! To possess her,—to hold her in my arms—heart to heart, lips to lips. . . this is what all the eternal forces of Nature meant when they made me man!"

And he watched with strained, passionate eyes the movements of the Princess Ziska as they grew slower and slower, till she seemed floating merely like a foam-bell on a wave, and then. . . from some unseen quarter of the room a rich throbbing voice began to sing:—

"Oh, for the passionless peace of the Lotus-Lily!
It floats in a waking dream on the waters chilly,
With its leaves unfurled
To the wondering world,
Knowing naught of the sorrow and restless pain
That burns and tortures the human brain;
Oh, for the passionless peace of the Lotus-Lily!
Oh, for the pure cold heart of the Lotus-Lily!
Bared to the moon on the waters dark and chilly.
A star above
Is its only love,
And one brief sigh of its scented breath
Is all it will ever know of Death;
Oh, for the pure cold heart of the Lotus-Lily!"

As the sound died away in a sigh rather than a note, the Princess Ziska's dancing ceased altogether. A shout of applause broke from all assembled, and in the midst of it there was a sudden commotion and excitement, and Dr. Dean was seen bending over a man's prostrate figure. The great French painter, Armand Gervase, had suddenly fainted.

XII

A curious yet very general feeling of superstitious uneasiness and discomfort pervaded the Gezireh Palace Hotel the day after the Princess Ziska's reception. Something had happened, and no one knew what. The proprieties had been outraged, but no one knew why. It was certainly not the custom for a hostess, and a Princess to boot, to dance like a wild bacchante before a crowd of her invited guests, yet, as Dr. Dean blandly observed,—

"Where was the harm? In London, ladies of good birth and breeding went in for 'skirt-dancing,' and no one presumed to breathe a word against their reputations; why in Cairo should not a lady go in for a Theban dance without being considered improper?"

Why, indeed? There seemed no adequate reason for being either surprised or offended; yet surprised and offended most people were, and scandal ran rife, and rumor wagged all its poisonous tongues to spread evil reports against the Princess Ziska's name and fame, till Denzil Murray, maddened and furious, rushed up to his sister in her room and swore that he would marry the Princess if he died for it.

"They are blackguarding her downstairs, the beasts!" he said hotly. "They are calling her by every bad name under the sun! But I will make everything straight for her; she shall be my wife! If she will have me, I will marry her to-morrow!"

Helen looked at him in speechless despair.

"Oh, Denzil!" she faltered, and then could say no more, for the tears that blinded her eyes.

"Oh, yes, of course, I know what you mean!" he continued, marching up and down the room excitedly. "You are like all the others; you think her an adventuress. I think her the purest, the noblest of women! There is where we differ. I spoke to her last night,—I told her I loved her."

"You did?" and Helen gazed at him with wet, tragic eyes,—"And she. . ."

"She bade me be silent. She told me I must not speak—not yet. She said she would give me her answer when we were all together at the Mena House Hotel."

"You intend to be one of the party there then?" said Helen faintly.

"Of course I do. And so do you, I hope."

"No, Denzil, I cannot. Don't ask me. I will stay here with Lady Fulkeward. She is not going, nor are the Chetwynd Lyles. I shall be quite safe with them. I would rather not go to the Mena House,—I could not bear it. . ."

Her voice gave way entirely, and she broke out crying bitterly.

Denzil stood still and regarded her with a kind of sullen shame and remorse.

"What a very sympathetic sister you are!" he observed. "When you see me madly in love with a woman—a perfectly beautiful, adorable woman—you put yourself at once in the way and make out that my marriage with her will be a misery to you. You surely do not expect me to remain single all my life, do you?"

"No, Denzil," sobbed Helen, "but I had hoped to see you marry some sweet girl of our own land who would be your dear and true companion,—who would be a sister to me,—who. . . there! don't mind me! Be happy in your own way, my dear brother. I have no business to interfere. I can only say that if the Princess Ziska consents to marry you, I will do my best to like her, for your sake."

"Well, that's something, at any rate," said Denzil, with an air of relief. "Don't cry, Helen, it bothers me. As for the 'sweet girl' you have got in view for me, you will permit me to say that 'sweet girls' are becoming uncommonly scarce in Britain. What with bicycle riders and great rough tomboys generally, with large hands and larger feet, I confess I do not care about them. I like a womanly woman,—a graceful woman,—a fascinating, bewitching woman, and the Princess is all that and more. Surely you consider her beautiful?"

"Very beautiful indeed!" sighed poor Helen.—"Too beautiful!"

"Nonsense! As if any woman can be too beautiful! I am sorry you won't come to the Mena House. It would be a change for you,—and Gervase is going."

"Is he better to-day?" inquired Helen timidly.

"Oh, I believe he is quite well again. It was the heat or the scent of the flowers, or something of that sort, that made him faint last night. He is not acclimatized yet, you know. And he said that the Princess's dancing made him giddy."

"I don't wonder at that," murmured Helen.

"It was marvellous—glorious!" said Denzil dreamily. "It was like nothing else ever seen or imagined!"

"If she were your wife, would you care for her to dance before people?" inquired Helen tremblingly.

Denzil turned upon her in haughty wrath.

"How like a woman that is! To insinuate a nasty suggestion—to imply an innuendo without uttering it! If she were my wife, she would do nothing unbecoming that position."

"Then you did think it a little unbecoming?" persisted Helen.

"No, I did Not!" said Denzil sharply. "An independent woman may do many things that a married woman may not. Marriage brings its own duties and responsibilities,—time enough to consider them when they come."

He turned angrily on his heel and left her, and Helen, burying her fair face in her hands, wept long and unrestrainedly. This "strange woman out of Egypt" had turned her brother's heart against her, and stolen away her almost declared lover. It was no wonder that her tears fell fast, wrung from her with the pain of this double wound; for Helen, though quiet and undemonstrative, had fine feelings and unsounded depths of passion in her nature, and the fatal attraction she felt for Armand Gervase was more powerful than she had herself known. Now that he had openly confessed his infatuation for another woman, it seemed as though the earth had opened at her feet and shown her nothing but a grave in which to fall. Life—empty and blank and bare of love and tenderness, stretched before her imagination; she saw herself toiling along the monotonously even road of duty till her hair became gray and her face thin and wan and wrinkled, and never a gleam again of the beautiful, glowing, romantic passion that for a short time had made her days splendid with the dreams that are sweeter than all realities.

Poor Helen! It was little marvel that she wept as all women weep when their hearts are broken. It is so easy to break a heart; sometimes a mere word will do it. But the vanishing of the winged Love-god from the soul is even more than heart-break,—it is utter and irretrievable loss,—complete and dominating chaos out of which no good thing can ever be designed or created. In our days we do our best to supply the place of a reluctant Eros by the gilded, grinning Mammon-figure which we try to consider as superior to any silver-pinioned god that ever descended in his rainbow car to sing heavenly songs to mortals; but it is an unlovely substitute,—a hideous idol at best; and grasp its golden knees and worship it as we will, it gives us little or no comfort in the hours of strong temptation or trouble. We have made a mistake—we, in our progressive generation,—we have banished the old sweetnesses, triumphs and delights of life, and we have got in exchange steam and electricity. But the heart of the age clamors on unsatisfied,—none of our "new" ideas content it—nothing pacifies its restless yearning; it feels—this great heart of human life—that it is losing more than it gains, hence the incessant, restless aching of the time, and the perpetual longing for something Science cannot teach,—something vague, beautiful, indefinable, yet satisfying to every pulse of the soul; and the nearest emotion to that divine solace is what we in our higher and better moments recognize as Love. And Love was lost to Helen Murray; the choice pearl had fallen in the vast gulf of Might-have-been, and not all the forces of Nature would ever restore to her that priceless gem.

And while she wept to herself in solitude, and her brother Denzil wandered about in the gardens of the hotel, encouraging within himself hopes of winning the bewitching Ziska for a wife, Armand Gervase, shut up in his room under plea of slight indisposition, reviewed the emotions of the past night and tired to analyze them. Some men are born self-analysts, and are able to dissect their feelings by some peculiar form of mental surgery which finally leads them to cut out tenderness as though it were a cancer, love as a disease, and romantic aspirations as mere uncomfortable growths injurious to self-interest, but Gervase was not one of these. Outwardly he assumed more or less the composed and careless demeanor of the modern French cynic, but inwardly the man was a raging fire of fierce passions which were sometimes too strong to be held in check. At the present moment he was prepared to sacrifice everything, even life itself, to obtain possession of the woman he coveted, and he made no attempt whatever to resist the tempest of desire that was urging him on with an invincible force in a direction which, for some strange and altogether inexplicable reason, he dreaded. Yes, there was a dim sense of terror lurking behind all the wild passion that filled his soul—a haunting, vague idea that this sudden love, with its glowing ardor and intoxicating delirium, was like the brilliant red sunset which frequently prognosticates a night of storm, ruin and death. Yet, though he felt this presentiment like a creeping shudder of cold through his blood, it did not hold him back, or for a moment impress him with the idea that it might be better to yield no further to this desperate love-madness which enthralled him.

Once only, he thought, "What if I left Egypt now—at once—and saw her no more?" And then he laughed scornfully at the impossibility proposed. "Leave Egypt!" he muttered, "I might as well leave the world altogether! She would draw me back with those sweet wild eyes of hers,—she would drag me from the uttermost parts of the earth to fall at her feet in a very agony of love. My God! She must have her way and do with me as she will, for I feel that she holds my life in her hands!"

As he spoke these last words half aloud, he sprang up from the chair in which he had been reclining, and stood for a moment lost in frowning meditation.

"My life in her hands!" he repeated musingly. "Yes, it has come to that! My life!" A great sigh broke from him. "My life—my art—my work—my name! In all these things I have taken pride, and she—she can trample them under her feet and make of me nothing more than man clamoring for woman's love! What a wild world it is! What a strange Force must that be which created it!—the Force that some men call God and others Devil! A strange, blind, brute Force!—for it makes us aspire only to fall; it gives a man dreams of ambition and splendid attainment only to fling him like a mad fool on a woman's breast, and bid him find there, and there only, the bewildering sweetness which makes everything else in existence poor and tame in comparison. Well, well—my life! What is it? A mere grain of sand dropped in the sea; let her do with it as she will. God! How I felt her power upon me last night,—last night when her lithe figure swaying in the dance reminded me. . ."

He paused, startled at the turn his own thoughts were taking.

"Of what? Let me try and express to myself now what I could not express or realize last night. She—Ziska—I thought was mine,—mine from her dimpled feet to her dusky hair,—and she danced for me alone. It seemed that the jewels she wore upon her rounded arms and slender ankles were all love-gifts from me—every circlet of gold, every starry, shining gem on her fair body was the symbol of some secret joy between us—joy so keen as to be almost pain. And as she danced, I thought I was in a vast hall of a majestic palace, where open colonnades revealed wide glimpses of a burning desert and deep blue sky. I heard the distant sound of rolling drums, and not far off I saw the Sphinx—a creature not old but new—resting upon a giant pedestal and guarding the sculptured gate of some great temple which contained, as I then thought, all the treasures of the world. I could paint the picture as I saw it then! It was a fleeting impression merely, conjured up by the dance that dizzied my brain. And that song of the Lotus-lily! That was strange—very strange, for I thought I had heard it often before,—and I saw myself in the vague dream, a prince, a warrior, almost a king, and far more famous in the world than I am now!"

He looked about him uneasily, with a kind of nervous terror, and his eyes rested for a moment on the easel where the picture he had painted of the Princess was placed, covered from view by a fold of dark cloth.

"Bah!" he exclaimed at last with a forced laugh, "What stupid fancies fool me! It is all the vague talk of that would-be learned ass, Dr. Dean, with his ridiculous theories about life and death. I shall be imagining I am his fad, Araxes, next! This sort of thing will never do. Let me reason out the matter calmly. I love this woman,—love her to absolute madness. It is not the best kind of love, maybe, but it is the only kind I am capable of, and such as it is, she possesses it all. What then? Well! We go to-morrow to the Pyramids, and we join her at the Mena House, I and the poor boy Denzil. He will try his chance—I mine. If he wins, I shall kill him as surely as I myself live,—yes, even though he is Helen's brother. No man shall snatch Ziska from my arms and continue to breathe. If I win, it is possible he may kill me, and I shall respect him for trying to do it. But I shall satisfy my love first; Ziska will be mine—mine in every sense of possession,—before I die. Yes, that must be—that will have to be. And afterwards,—why let Denzil do his worst; a man can but die once."

He drew the cloth off his easel and stared at the strange picture of the Princess, which seemed almost sentient in its half-watchful, half-mocking expression.

"There is a dead face and a living one on this canvas," he said, "and the dead face seems to enthral me as much as the living. Both have the same cruel smile,—both the same compelling magnetism of eye. Only it is a singular thing that I should know the dead face even more intimately than the living—that the tortured look upon it should be a kind of haunting memory—horrible—ghastly. . ."

He flung the cloth over the easel again impatiently, and tried to laugh at his own morbid imagination.

"I know who is responsible for all this nonsense," he said. "It is that ridiculous little half-mad faddist, Dr. Dean. He is going to the Mena House, too. Well!—he will be the witness of a comedy or a tragedy there,—and Heaven alone knows which it will be!"

And to distract his thoughts from dwelling any longer on the haunting ideas that perplexed him, he took up one of the latest and frothiest of French novels and began to read. Some one in a room not far off was singing a French song,—a man with a rich baritone voice,—and unconsciously to himself Gervase caught the words as they rang out full and clearly on the quiet, heated air—

> *O toi que j'ai tant aimee*
> *Songes-tu que je t'aime encor?*
> *Et dans ton ame alarmee,*
> *Ne sens-tu pas quelque remord?*
> *Viens avec moi, si tu m'aimes,*
> *Habiter dans ces deserts;*
> *Nous y vivrons pour nous memes,*
> *Oublies de tout l'univers!*

And something like a mist of tears clouded his aching eyes as he repeated, half mechanically and dreamily—

> *O toi que j'ai tant aimee,*
> *Songes-tu que je t'aime encor?*

XIII

For the benefit of those among the untravelled English who have not yet broken a soda-water bottle against the Sphinx, or eaten sandwiches to the immortal memory of Cheops, it may be as well to explain that the Mena House Hotel is a long, rambling, roomy building, situated within five minutes' walk of the Great Pyramid, and happily possessed of a golfing-ground and a marble swimming-bath. That ubiquitous nuisance, the "amateur photographer," can there have his "dark room" for the development of his more or less imperfect "plates"; and there is a resident chaplain for the piously inclined. With a chaplain and a "dark room," what more can the aspiring soul of the modern tourist desire? Some of the rooms at the Mena House are small and stuffy; others large and furnished with sufficient elegance: and the Princess Ziska had secured a "suite" of the best that could be obtained, and was soon installed there with befitting luxury. She left Cairo quite suddenly, and without any visible preparation, the morning after the reception in which she had astonished her guests by her dancing: and she did not call at the Gezireh Palace Hotel to say good-bye to any of her acquaintances there. She was perhaps conscious that her somewhat "free" behavior had startled several worthy and sanctimonious persons; and possibly she also thought that to take rooms in an hotel which was only an hour's distance from Cairo, could scarcely be considered as absenting herself from Cairene society. She was followed to her desert retreat by Dr. Dean, Armand Gervase, and Denzil Murray, who drove to the Mena House together in one carriage, and were more or less all three in a sober and meditative frame of mind. They arrived in time to see the Sphinx bathed in the fierce glow of an ardent sunset, which turned the golden sands to crimson, and made the granite monster look like a cruel idol surrounded by a sea of blood. The brilliant red of the heavens flamed in its stony eyes, and gave them a sentient look as of contemplated murder,—and the same radiance fitfully playing on the half-scornful, half-sensual lips caused them to smile with a seeming voluptuous mockery. Dr. Dean stood transfixed for a while at the strange splendor of the spectacle, and turning to his two silent companions, said suddenly:

"There is something, after all, in the unguessed riddle of the Sphinx. It is not a fable; it is a truth. There is a problem to be solved, and that monstrous creature knows it! The woman's face, the brute's body—Spiritualism and Materialism in one! It is life, and more than life; it is love. Forever and forever it teaches the same wonderful, terrible mystery. We aspire, yet we fall; love would fain give us wings wherewith to fly; but the wretched body lies prone—supine; it cannot soar to the Light Eternal."

"What Is the Light Eternal?" queried Gervase, moodily. "How do we know it exists? We cannot prove it. This world is what we see; we have to do with it and ourselves. Soul without body could not exist. . ."

"Could it not?" said the Doctor. "How, then, does body exist without soul?"

This was an unexpected but fair question, and Gervase found himself curiously perplexed by it. He offered no reply, neither did Denzil, and they all three slowly entered the Mena House Hotel, there to be met with deferential salutations by the urbane and affable landlord, and to be assured that they would find their rooms comfortable, and also that "Madame la Princesse Ziska" expected them to dine with her that evening. At this message, Denzil Murray made a sign to Gervase that he wished to speak to him alone. Gervase move aside with him.

"Give me my chance!" said Denzil, fiercely.

"Take it!" replied Gervase listlessly. "Let to-night witness the interchange of hearts between you and the Princess; I shall not interfere."

Denzil stared at him in sullen astonishment.

"You will not interfere? Your fancy for her is at an end?"

Gervase raised his dark, glowing eyes and fixed them on his would-be rival with a strange and sombre expression.

"My 'fancy' for her? My good boy, take care what you say! Don't rouse me too far, for I am dangerous! My 'fancy' for her! What do you know of it? You are hot-blooded and young; but the chill of the North controls you in a fashion, while I—a man in the prime of manhood—am of the South, and the Southern fire brooks no control. Have you seen a quiet ocean, smooth as glass, with only a dimple in the deep blue to show that perhaps, should occasion serve, there might arise a little wave? And have you seen the wild storm breaking from a black cloud and suddenly making that quiet expanse nothing but a tourbillon of furious elements, in which the very sea-gull's cry is whelmed and lost in the thunder of the billows? Such a storm as that may be compared to the 'fancy' you suppose I feel for the woman who has dragged us both here to die at her feet—for that, I believe, is what it will come to.

Life is not possible under the strain of emotion with which we two are living it. . ."

He broke off, then resumed in quieter tones:

"I say to you: Use your opportunities while you have them. After dinner I will leave you alone with the Princess. I will go out for a stroll with Dr. Dean. Take your chance, Denzil, for, as I live, it is your last! It will be my turn next! Give me credit for to-night's patience!"

He turned quickly away, and in a moment was gone. Denzil Murray stood still for a while, thinking deeply, and trying to review the position in which he found himself. He was madly in love with a woman for whom his only sister had the most violent antipathy; and that sister, who had once been all in all to him, had now become almost less than nothing in the headstrong passion which consumed him. No consideration for her peace and ultimate happiness affected him, though he was sensible of a certain remorseful pity when thinking of her gentle ways and docile yielding to his often impatient and impetuous humors; but, after all, she was only his sister,—she could not understand his present condition of mind. Then there was Gervase, whom he had for some years looked upon as one of his most admired and intimate friends; now he was nothing more or less than a rival and an enemy, notwithstanding his seeming courtesy and civil self-restraint. As a matter of fact, he, Denzil, was left alone to face his fate: to dare the brilliant seduction of the witching eyes of Ziska,—to win her or to lose her forever! And consider every point as he would, the weary conviction was borne in upon him that, whether he met with victory or defeat, the result would bring more misery than joy.

When he entered the Princess's salon that evening, he found Dr. Dean and Gervase already there. The Princess herself, attired in a dinner-dress made with quite a modern Parisian elegance, received him in her usual graceful manner, and expressed with much sweetness her hope that the air of the desert would prove beneficial to him after the great heats that had prevailed in Cairo. Nothing but conventionalities were spoken. Oh, those conventionalities! What a world of repressed emotions they sometimes cover! How difficult it is to conceive that the man and woman who are greeting each other with calm courtesy in a crowded drawing-room are the very two, who, standing face to face in the moonlit silence of some lonely grove of trees or shaded garden, once in their lives suddenly realized the wild passion that neither dared confess! Tragedies lie deepest under conventionalities—such secrets are buried beneath them as sometimes might make the angels weep! They are safeguards, however, against stronger emotions; and the strange bathos of two human creatures talking politely about the weather when the soul of each is clamoring for the other, has sometimes, despite its absurdity, saved the situation.

At dinner, the Princess Ziska devoted herself almost entirely to the entertainment of Dr. Dean, and awakened his interest very keenly on the subject of the Great Pyramid.

"It has never really been explored," she said. "The excavators who imagine they have fathomed its secrets are completely in error. The upper chambers are mere deceits to the investigator; they were built and planned purposely to mislead, and the secrets they hide have never even been guessed at, much less discovered."

"Are you sure of that?" inquired the Doctor, eagerly. "If so, would you not give your information. . ."

"I neither give my information nor sell it," interrupted the Princess, smiling coldly. "I am only a woman—and women are supposed to know nothing. With the rest of my sex, I am judged illogical and imaginative; you wise men would call my knowledge of history deficient, my facts not proven. But, if you like, I will tell you the story of the construction of the Great Pyramid, and why it is unlikely that anyone will ever find the treasures that are buried within it. You can receive the narrative with the usual incredulity common to men; I shall not attempt to argue the pros and cons with you, because I never argue. Treat it as a fairy-tale—no woman is ever supposed to know anything for a fact,—she is too stupid. Only men are wise!"

Her dark, disdainful glance flashed on Gervase and Denzil; anon she smiled bewitchingly, and added:

"Is it not so?"

"Wisdom is nothing compared to beauty," said Gervase. "A beautiful woman can turn the wisest man into a fool."

The Princess laughed lightly.

"Yes, and a moment afterwards he regrets his folly," she said. "He clamors for the beautiful woman as a child might cry for the moon, and when he at last possesses her, he tires. Satisfied with having compassed her degradation, he exclaims: 'What shall I do with this beauty, which, because it is mine, now palls upon me? Let me kill it and forget it; I am aweary of love, and the world is full of women!' That is the way of your sex, Monsieur Gervase; it is a brutal way, but it is the one most of you follow."

"There is such a thing as love!" said Denzil, looking up quickly, a pained flush on his handsome face.

"In the hearts of women, yes!" said Ziska, her voice growing tremulous with strange and sudden passion. "Women love—ah!—with what force and tenderness and utter abandonment of self! But their love is in ninety-nine cases out of a hundred utterly wasted; it is a largesse flung to the ungrateful, a jewel tossed in the mire! If there were not some compensation in the next life for the ruin wrought on loving women, the Eternal God himself would be a mockery and a jest."

"And is he not?" queried Gervase, ironically. "Fair Princess, I would not willingly shake your faith in things unseen, but what does the 'Eternal God,' as you call Him, care as to the destiny of any individual unit on this globe of matter? Does He interfere when the murderer's knife descends upon the victim? And has He ever interfered? He it is who created the sexes and placed between them the strong attraction that often works more evil and misery than good; and what barrier has He ever interposed between woman and man, her natural destroyer? None!—save the trifling one of virtue, which is a flimsy thing, and often breaks down at the first temptation. No, my dear Princess; the 'Eternal God,' if there is one, does nothing but look on impassively at the universal havoc of creation. And in the blindness and silence of things, I cannot recognize an Eternal God at all; we were evidently made to eat, drink, breed and die—and there an end."

"What of ambition?" asked Dr. Dean. "What of the inspiration that lifts a man beyond himself and his material needs, and teaches him to strive after the Highest?"

"Mere mad folly!" replied Gervase impetuously. "Take the Arts. I, for example, dream of painting a picture that shall move the world to admiration,—but I seldom grasp the idea I have imagined. I paint something,—anything,—and the world gapes at it, and some rich fool buys it, leaving me free to paint another something; and so on and so on, to the end of my career. I ask you what satisfaction does it bring? What is it to Raphael that thousands of human units, cultured and silly, have stared at his 'Madonnas' and his famous Cartoons?"

"Well, we do not exactly know what it may or may not be to Raphael," said the Doctor, meditatively. "According to my theories, Raphael is not dead, but merely removed into another form, on another planet possibly, and is working elsewhere. You might as well ask what it is to Araxes now that he was a famous warrior once?"

Gervase moved uneasily.

"You have got Araxes on the brain, Doctor," he said, with a forced smile, "and in our conversation we are forgetting that the Princess has promised to tell us a fairytale, the story of the Great Pyramid."

The Princess looked at him, then at Denzil Murray, and lastly at Dr. Dean.

"Would you really care to hear it?" she asked.

"Most certainly!" they all three answered.

She rose from the dinner-table.

"Come here to the window," she said. "You can see the great structure now, in the dusky light,—look at it well and try, if you can, to realize that deep, deep down in the earth on which it stands is a connected gallery of rocky caves wherein no human foot has ever penetrated since the Deluge swept over the land and made a desert of all the old-time civilization!"

Her slight figure appeared to dilate as she spoke, raising one slender hand and arm to point at the huge mass that towered up against the clear, starlit sky. Her listeners were silent, awed and attentive.

"One of the latest ideas concerning the Pyramids is, as you know, that they were built as towers of defence against the Deluge. That is correct. The wise men of the old days foretold the time when 'the waters should rise and cover the earth,' and these huge monuments were prepared and raised to a height which it was estimated would always appear above the level of the coming flood, to show where the treasures of Egypt were hidden for safety. Yes,—the treasures of Egypt, the wisdom, the science of Egypt! They are all down there still! And there, to all intents and purposes, they are likely to remain."

"But archaeologists are of the opinion that the Pyramids have been thoroughly explored," began Dr. Dean, with some excitement.

The Princess interrupted him by a slight gesture.

"Archaeologists, my dear Doctor, are like the rest of this world's so-called 'learned' men; they work in one groove, and are generally content with it. Sometimes an unusually brilliant brain conceives the erratic notion of working in several grooves, and is straightway judged as mad or fanatic. It is when these comet-like intelligences sweep across the world's horizon that we hear of a Julius Caesar, a Napoleon, a Shakespeare. But archaeologists are the narrowest and dryest of men,—they preconceive a certain system of work and follow it out by mathematical rule and plan, without one touch of imagination to help them to discover new channels of interest or historical information. As I told you before I began to speak, you are welcome to entirely disbelieve my story of the Great Pyramid,—but as I have begun it, you may as well hear it through." She paused a moment, then went on: "According to my information, the building of the Pyramids was commenced three hundred years before the Deluge, in the time of Saurid, the son of Sabaloc, who, it is said, was the first to receive a warning dream of the coming flood. Saurid, being convinced by his priests, astrologers and soothsayers that the portent was a true one, became from that time possessed of one idea, which was that the vast learning of Egypt, its sciences, discoveries and strange traditions should not be lost,—and that the exploits and achievements of those who were great and famous in the land should be so recorded as never to be forgotten. In those days, here where you see these measureless tracts of sand, there were great mountainous rocks and granite quarries, and Saurid utilized these for the hollowing out of deep caverns in which to conceal treasure. When these caverns were prepared to his liking, he caused a floor to be made, portions of which were rendered movable by means of secret springs, and then leaving a hollow space of some four feet in height, he started foundations for another floor above it. This upper floor is what you nowadays see when you enter the Pyramid,—and no one imagines that under it is an open space with room to walk in, and yet another floor below, where everything of value is secreted."

Dr. Dean drew a long breath of wonderment.

"Astonishing, if true!"

The Princess smiled somewhat disdainfully, and went on:

"Saurid's work was carried on after his death by his successors, and with thousands of slaves toiling night and day the Pyramids were in the course of years raised above the caverns which concealed Egypt's mysteries. Everything was gradually accumulated in these underground store-houses,—the engraved talismans, the slabs of stone on which were deeply carved the geometrical and astronomical sciences; indestructible glass chests containing papyri, on which were written the various discoveries made in beneficial drugs, swift poisons, and other medicines. And among these many things were thirty great jars full of precious stones, some of which were marvels of the earth. They are there still! And some of the great men who died were interred in these caves, every one in a separate chamber inlaid with gold and gems, and I think," here the

Princess turned her dark eyes full on Dr. Dean, "I think that if you knew the secret way of lifting the apparently immovable floor, which is like the solid ground, and descending through the winding galleries beneath, it is more than probable you would find in the Great Pyramid the tomb of Araxes!"

Her eyes glistened strangely in the evening light with that peculiar fiery glow which had made Dr. Dean once describe them as being like the eyes of a vampire-bat, and there was something curiously impressive in her gesture as she once more pointed to the towering structure which loomed against the heavens, with one star flashing immediately above it. A sudden involuntary shudder shook Gervase as with icy cold; he moved restlessly, and presently remarked:

"Well, it is a safe tomb, at any rate! Whoever Araxes was, he stands little chance of being exhumed if he lies two floors below the Great Pyramid in a sealed-up rocky cavern! Princess, you look like an inspired prophetess!—so much talk of ancient and musty times makes me feel uncanny, and I will, with your permission, have a smoke with Dr. Dean in the garden to steady my nerves. The mere notion of thirty vases of unclaimed precious stones hidden down yonder is enough to upset any man's equanimity!"

"The papyri would interest me more than the jewels," said Dr. Dean. "What do you say, Denzil?"

Denzil Murray woke up suddenly from a fit of abstraction.

"Oh, I don't know anything about it," he answered. "I never was very much interested in those old times,—they seem to me all myth. I could never link past, present and future together as some people can; they are to me all separate things. The past is done with,—the present is our own to enjoy or to detest, and the future no man can look into."

"Ah, Denzil, you are young, and reflection has not been very hard at work in that headstrong brain of yours," said Dr. Dean with an indulgent smile, "otherwise you would see that past, present and future are one and indissoluble. The past is as much a part of your present identity as the present, and the future, too, lies in you in embryo. The mystery of one man's life contains all mysteries, and if we could only understand it from its very beginning we should find out the cause of all things, and the ultimate intention of creation."

"Well, now, you have all had enough serious talk," said the Princess Ziska lightly, "so let us adjourn to the drawing-room. One of my waiting-women shall sing to you by and by; she has a very sweet voice."

"Is it she who sings that song about the lotus-lily?" asked Gervase, suddenly.

The Princess smiled strangely.

"Yes,—it is she."

Dr. Dean chose a cigar from a silver box on the table; Gervase did the same.

"Won't you smoke, Denzil?" he asked carelessly.

"No, thanks!" Denzil spoke hurriedly and hoarsely. "I think—if the Princess will permit me—I will stay and talk with her in the drawing-room while you two have your smoke together."

The Princess gave a charming bow of assent to this proposition. Gervase took the Doctor somewhat roughly by the arm and led him out through the open French window into the grounds beyond, remarking as he went:

"You will excuse us, Princess? We leave you in good company!"

She smiled.

"I will excuse you, certainly! But do not be long!"

And she passed from the dining-room into the small saloon beyond, followed closely by Denzil.

Once out in the grounds, Gervase gave vent to a boisterous fit of wild laughter, so loud and fierce that little Dr. Dean came to an abrupt standstill, and stared at him in something of alarm as well as amazement.

"Are you going mad, Gervase?" he asked.

"Yes!" cried Gervase, "that is just it,—I am going mad,—mad for love, or whatever you please to call it! What do you think I am made of? Flesh and blood, or cast-iron? Heavens! Do you think if all the elements were to combine in a war against me, they should cheat me out of this woman or rob me of her? No, no! A thousand times no! Satisfy yourself, my excellent Doctor, with your musty records of the past,—prate as you choose of the future,—but in the immediate, burning, active present my will is law! And the fool Denzil thinks to thwart me,—I, who have never been thwarted since I knew the meaning of existence!"

He paused in a kind of breathless agitation, and Dr. Dean grasped his arm firmly.

"Come, come, what is all this excitement for?" he said. "What are you saying about Denzil?"

Gervase controlled himself with a violent effort and forced a smile.

"He has got his chance,—I have given it to him! He is alone with the Princess, and he is asking her to be his wife!"

"Nonsense!" said the Doctor sharply. "If he does commit such a folly, it will be no use. The woman is NOT HUMAN!"

"Not human?" echoed Gervase, his black eyes dilating with a sudden amazement—"What do you mean?"

The little Doctor rubbed his nose impatiently and seemed sorry he had spoken.

"I mean—let me see! What do I mean?" he said at last meditatively—"Oh, well, it is easy enough of explanation. There are plenty of people like the Princess Ziska to whom I would apply the words 'not human.' She is all beauty and no heart. Again—if you follow me—she is all desire and no passion, which is a character 'like unto the beasts which perish.' A large majority of men are made so, and some women,—though the women are comparatively few. Now, so far as the Princess Ziska is concerned," continued the Doctor, fixing his keen, penetrative glance on Gervase as he spoke, "I frankly admit to you that I find in her material for a very curious and complex study. That is why I have come after her here. I have said she is all desire and no passion. That of itself is inhuman; but what I am busy about now is to try and analyze the nature of the particular desire that moves her, controls her, keeps her alive,—in short. It is not love; of that I feel confident; and it is not hate,— though it is more like hate than love. It is something indefinable, something that is almost occult, so deep-seated and bewildering is the riddle. You look upon me as a madman—yes! I know you do! But mad or sane, I emphatically repeat, the Princess is NOT HUMAN, and by this expression I wish to imply that though she has the outward appearance of a most beautiful and seductive human body, she has the soul of a fiend. Now, do you understand me?"

"It would take Oedipus himself all his time to do that,"—said Gervase, forcing a laugh which had no mirth in it, for he was conscious of a vaguely unpleasant sensation—a chill, as of some dark presentiment, which oppressed his mind. "When you know I do not believe in the soul, why do you talk to me about it? The soul of a fiend,—the soul of an angel,—what are they? Mere empty terms to me, meaning nothing. I think I agree with you though, in one or two points concerning the Princess; par exemple, I do not look upon her as one of those delicately embodied purities of womanhood before whom we men instinctively bend in reverence, but whom, at the same time, we generally avoid, ashamed of our vileness. No; she is certainly not one of the

> *"Maiden roses left to die*
> *Because they climb so near the sky,*
> *That not the boldest passer-by*
> *Can pluck them from their vantage high.'*

And whether it is best to be a solitary 'maiden-rose' or a Princess Ziska, who shall say? And human or inhuman, whatever composition she is made of, you may make yourself positively certain that Denzil Murray is just now doing his best to persuade her to be a Highland chatelaine in the future. Heavens, what a strange fate it will be for la belle Egyptienne!"

"Oh, you think she Is Egyptian then?" queried Dr. Dean, with an air of lively curiosity.

"Of course I do. She has the Egyptian type of form and countenance. Consider only the resemblance between her and the dancer she chose to represent the other night—the Ziska-Charmazel of the antique sculpture on her walls!"

"Ay, but if you grant one resemblance, you must also admit another," said the Doctor quickly. "The likeness between yourself and the old-world warrior, Araxes, is no less remarkable!" Gervase moved uneasily, and a sudden pallor blanched his face, making it look wan and haggard in the light of the rising moon. "And it is rather singular," went on the imperturbable savant, "that according to the legend or history—whichever you please to consider it,—for in time, legends become histories and histories legends—Araxes should have been the lover of this very Ziska-Charmazel, and that you, who are the living portrait of Araxes, should suddenly become enamored of the equally living portrait of the dead woman! You must own, that to a mere onlooker and observer like myself, it seems a curious coincidence!"

Gervase smoked on in silence, his level brows contracted in a musing frown.

"Yes, it seems curious," he said at last, "but a great many curious coincidences happen in this world—so many that we, in our days of rush and turmoil, have not time to consider them as they come or go. Perhaps of all the strange things in life, the sudden sympathies and the headstrong passions which spring up in a day or a night between certain men and certain women are the strangest. I look upon you, Doctor, as a very clever fellow with just a little twist in his brain, or let us say a 'fad' about spiritual matters; but in one of your more or less fantastic and extravagant theories I am half disposed to believe, and that is the notion you have of the possibility of some natures, male and female, having met before in a previous state of existence and under different forms, such as birds, flowers, or forest animals, or even mere incorporeal breaths of air and flame. It is an idea which I confess fascinates me. It seems fairly reasonable too, for, as many scientists argue that you cannot destroy matter, but only transform it, there is really nothing impossible in the suggestion."

He paused, then added slowly as he flung the end of his cigar away:

"I have felt the force of this odd fancy of yours most strongly since I met the Princess Ziska."

"Indeed! Then the impression she gave you first is still upon you— that of having known her before?"

Gervase waited a minute or two before replying; then he answered:

"Yes. And not only of having known her before, but of having loved her before. Love!—mon Dieu!—what a tame word it is! How poorly it expresses the actual emotion! Fire in the veins—delirium in the brain— reason gone to chaos! And this madness is mildly described as 'love?'"

"There are other words for it," said the Doctor. "Words that are not so poetic, but which, perhaps, are more fitting."

"No!" interrupted Gervase, almost fiercely. "There are no words which truly describe this one emotion which rules the world. I know what You mean, of course; you mean evil words, licentious words, and yet it has nothing whatever to do with these. You cannot call such an exalted state of the nerves and sensations by an evil name."

Dr. Dean pondered the question for a few moments.

"No, I am not sure that I can," he said, meditatively. "If I did, I should have to give an evil name to the Creator who designed man and woman and ordained the law of attraction which draws, and often DRAGS them together. I like to be fair to everybody, the Creator included; yet to be fair to everybody I shall appear to sanction immorality. For the fact is that our civilization has upset all the original intentions of nature. Nature evidently meant Love, or the emotion we call Love, to be the keynote of the universe. But apparently Nature did not intend marriage. The flowers, the birds, the lower animals, mate afresh every spring, and this is the creed that the disciples of Naturalism nowadays are anxious to force upon the attention of the world. It is only men and women, they say, that are so foolish as to take each other for better or worse till death

MARIE CORELLI

do them part. Now, I should like, from the physical scientist's point of view, to prove that the men and women are wrong, and that the lower animals are right; but spiritual science comes in and confutes me. For in spiritual science I find this truth, which will not be gainsaid—namely, that from time immemorial, certain immortal forms of Nature have been created solely for one another; like two halves of a circle, they are intended to meet and form the perfect round, and all the elements of creation, spiritual and material, will work their hardest to pull them together. Such natures, I consider, should absolutely and imperatively be joined in marriage. It then becomes a divine decree. Even grant, if you like, that the natures so joined are evil, and that the sympathy between them is of a more or less reprehensible character, it is quite as well that they should unite, and that the result of such an union should be seen. The evil might come out of them in a family of criminals which the law could exterminate with advantage to the world in general. Whereas on the other hand, given two fine and aspiring natures with perfect sympathy between them, as perfect as the two notes of a perfect chord, the children of such a marriage would probably be as near gods as humanity could bring them. I speak as a scientist merely. Such consequences are not foreseen by the majority, and marriages as a rule take place between persons who are by no means made for each other. Besides, a kind of devil comes into the business, and often prevents the two sympathetic natures conjoining. Love-matters alone are quite sufficient to convince me that there Is a devil as well as a divinity that 'shapes our ends.'"

"You speak as if you yourself had loved, Doctor," said Gervase, with a half smile.

"And so I have," replied the Doctor, calmly. "I have loved to the full as passionately and ardently as even you can love. I thank God the woman I loved died,—I could never have possessed her, for she was already wedded,—and I would not have disgraced her by robbing her from her lawful husband. So Death stepped in and gave her to me— forever!" and he raised his eyes to the solemn starlit sky. "Yes, nothing can ever come between us now; no demon tears her white soul from me; she died innocent of evil, and she is mine—mine in every pulse of her being, as we shall both know hereafter!"

His face, which was not remarkable for any beauty of feature, grew rapt and almost noble in its expression, and Gervase looked at him with a faint touch of ironical wonder.

"Upon my word, your morality almost outreaches your mysticism!" he said. "I see you are one of those old-fashioned men who think marriage a sacred sort of thing and the only self-respecting form of love."

"Old-fashioned I may be," replied Dr. Dean; "but I certainly believe in marriage for the woman's sake. If the license of men were not restrained by some sort of barrier it would break all bounds. Now I, had I chosen, could have taken the woman I loved to myself; it needed but a little skilful persuasion on my part, for her husband was a drink-sodden ruffian. . ."

"And why, in the name of Heaven, did you not do so?" demanded Gervase impatiently.

"Because I know the end of all such liaisons," said the Doctor sadly. "A month or two of delirious happiness, then years of remorse to follow. The man is lowered in his own secret estimation of himself, and the woman is hopelessly ruined, socially and morally. No, Death is far better; and in my case Death has proved a good friend, for it has given me the spotless soul of the woman I loved, which is far fairer than her body was."

"But, unfortunately, intangible!" said Gervase, satirically.

The Doctor looked at him keenly and coldly.

"Do not be too sure of that, my friend! Never talk about what you do not understand; you only wander astray. The spiritual world is a blank to you, so do not presume to judge of what you will never realize TILL REALIZATION IS FORCED UPON YOU!"

He uttered the last words with slow and singular emphasis.

"Forced upon me?" began Gervase. "What do you mean? . . ."

He broke off abruptly, for at that moment Denzil Murray emerged from the doorway of the hotel, and came towards them with an unsteady, swaying step like that of a drunken man.

"You had better go in to the Princess," he said, staring at Gervase with a wild smile; "she is waiting for you!"

"What's the matter with you, Denzil?" inquired Dr. Dean, catching him by the arm as he made a movement to go on and pass them.

Denzil stopped, frowning impatiently.

"Matter? Nothing! What should be the matter?"

"Oh, no offence; no offence, my boy!" and Dr. Dean at once loosened his arm. "I only thought you looked as if you had had some upset or worry, that's all."

"Climate! climate!" said Denzil, hoarsely. "Egypt does not agree with me, I suppose!—the dryness of the soil breeds fever and a touch of

madness! Men are not blocks of wood or monoliths of stone; they are creatures of flesh and blood, of nerve and muscle; you cannot torture them so. . ."

He interrupted himself with a kind of breathless irritation at his own speech. Gervase regarded him steadily, slightly smiling.

"Torture them how, Denzil?" asked the Doctor, kindly. "Dear lad, you are talking nonsense. Come and stroll with me up and down; the air is quite balmy and delightful; it will cool your brain."

"Yes, it needs cooling!" retorted Denzil, beginning to laugh with a sort of wild hilarity. "Too much wine,—too much woman,—too much of these musty old-world records and ghastly pyramids!"

Here he broke off, adding quickly:

"Doctor, Helen and I will go back to England next week, if all is well."

"Why, certainly, certainly!" said Dr. Dean, soothingly. "I think we are all beginning to feel we have had enough of Egypt. I shall probably return home with you. Meanwhile, come for a stroll and talk to me; Monsieur Armand Gervase will perhaps go in and excuse us for a few minutes to the Princess Ziska."

"With pleasure!" said Gervase; then, beckoning Denzil Murray aside, he whispered:

"Tell me, have you won or lost?"

"Lost!" replied Denzil, fiercely, through his set teeth. "It is your turn now! But, if you win, as sure as there is a God above us, I will kill you!"

"Soit! But not till I am ready for killing! After To-Morrow Night I shall be at your service, not till then!"

And smiling coldly, his dark face looking singularly pale and stern in the moonlight, Gervase turned away, and, walking with his usual light, swift, yet leisurely tread, entered the Princess's apartment by the French window which was still open, and from which the sound of sweet music came floating deliciously on the air as he disappeared.

XIV

In a half-reclining attitude of indolently graceful ease, the Princess Ziska watched from beneath the slumbrous shadow of her long-fringed eyelids the approach of her now scarcely-to-be controlled lover. He came towards her with a certain impetuosity of movement which was so far removed from ordinary conventionality as to be wholly admirable from the purely picturesque point of view, despite the fact that it expressed more passion and impatience than were in keeping with nineteenth-century customs and manners. He had almost reached her side before he became aware that there were two other women in the room besides the Princess,—silent, veiled figures that sat, or rather crouched, on the floor, holding quaintly carved and inlaid musical instruments of some antique date in their hands, the only sign of life about them being their large, dark, glistening almond-shaped eyes, which were every now and then raised and fixed on Gervase with an intense and searching look of inquiry. Strangely embarrassed by their glances, he addressed the Princess in a low tone:

"Will you not send away your women?"

She smiled.

"Yes, presently; if you wish it, I will. But you must hear some music first. Sit down there," and she pointed with her small jewelled hand to a low chair near her own. "My lutist shall sing you something,—in English, of course!—for all the world is being Anglicized by degrees, and there will soon be no separate nations left. Something, too, of romantic southern passion is being gradually grafted on to English sentiment, so that English songs are not so stupid as they were once. I translated some stanzas from one of the old Egyptian poets into English the other day, perhaps you will like them. Myrmentis, sing us the 'Song of Darkness.'"

An odd sensation of familiarity with the name of "Myrmentis" startled Gervase as he heard it pronounced, and he looked at the girl who was so called in a kind of dread. But she did not meet his questioning regard,—she was already bending over her lute and tuning its strings, while her companion likewise prepared to accompany her on a similar though larger instrument, and in an-other moment her voice, full and rich, with a sobbing passion in it which thrilled him to the inmost soul, rang out on the warm silence:

MARIE CORELLI

In the darkness what deeds are done!
What wild words spoken!
What joys are tasted, what passion wasted!
What hearts are broken!
Not a glimpse of the moon shall shine,
Not a star shall mark
The passing of night,—or shed its light
On my Dream of the Dark!

On the scented and slumbrous air,
Strange thoughts are thronging;
And a blind desire more fierce than fire
Fills the soul with longing;
Through the silence heavy and sweet
Comes the panting breath
Of a lover unseen from the Might-Have-Been,
Whose loving is Death!

In the darkness a deed was done,
A wild word spoken!
A joy was tasted,—a passion wasted,—
A heart was broken!
Not a glimpse of the moon shall shine,
Not a star shall mark
The passing of night,—or shed its light
On my Dream of the Dark!

The song died away in a shuddering echo, and before Gervase had time to raise his eyes from their brooding study of the floor the singer and her companion had noiselessly disappeared, and he was left alone with the Princess Ziska. He drew along breath, and turning fully round in his chair, looked at her steadily. There was a faint smile on her lips—a smile of mingled mockery and triumph,—her beautiful witch-like eyes glittered. Leaning towards her, he grasped her hands suddenly in his own.

"Now," he whispered, "shall I speak or be silent?"

"Whichever you please," she responded composedly, still smiling. "Speech or silence rest equally with yourself. I compel neither."

"That is false!" he said passionately. "You do compel! Your eyes drag my very soul out of me—your touch drives me into frenzy! You temptress! You force me to speak, though you know already what I have to say! That I love you, love you! And that you love me! That your whole life leaps to mine as mine to yours! You know all this; if I were stricken dumb, you could read it in my face, but you will have it spoken—you will extort from me the whole secret of my madness!—yes, for you to take a cruel joy in knowing that I AM mad—mad for the love of you! And you cannot be too often or too thoroughly assured that your own passion finds its reflex in me!"

He paused, abruptly checked in his wild words by the sound of her low, sweet, chill laughter. She withdrew her hands from his burning grasp.

"My dear friend," she said lightly, "you really have a very excellent opinion of yourself—excuse me for saying so! 'My own passion!' Do you actually suppose I have a 'passion' for you?" And rising from her chair, she drew up her slim supple figure to its full height and looked at him with an amused and airy scorn. "You are totally mistaken! No one man living can move me to love; I know all men too well! Their natures are uniformly composed of the same mixture of cruelty, lust and selfishness; and forever and forever, through all the ages of the world, they use the greater part of their intellectual abilities in devising new ways to condone and conceal their vices. You call me 'temptress';—why? The temptation, if any there be, emanates from yourself and your own unbridled desires; I do nothing. I am made as I am made; if my face or my form seems fair in your eyes, this is not my fault. Your glance lights on me, as the hawk's lights on coveted prey; but think you the prey loves the hawk in response? It is the mistake all men make with all women,—to judge them always as being of the same base material as themselves. Some women there are who shame their womanhood; but the majority, as a rule, preserve their self-respect till taught by men to lose it."

Gervase sprang up and faced her, his eyes flashing dangerously.

"Do not make any pretence with me!" he said half angrily. "Never tell me you cannot love! . . ."

"I HAVE loved!" she interrupted him. "As true women love,—once, and only once. It suffices; not for one lifetime, but many. I loved; and gave myself ungrudgingly and trustingly to the man my soul worshipped. I was betrayed, of course!—it is the usual story—quite old, quite commonplace! I can tell it to you without so much as a blush of pain! Since then I have not loved,—I have HATED; and I live but for one thing—Revenge."

MARIE CORELLI

Her face paled as she spoke, and a something vague, dark, spectral and terrible seemed to enfold her like a cloud where she stood. Anon she smiled sweetly, and with a bewitching provocativeness.

"Your 'passion,' you see, my friend awakens rather a singular 'reflex' in me!—not quite of the nature you imagined!"

He remained for a moment inert; then, with an almost savage boldness, threw his arm about her.

"Have everything your own way, Ziska!" he said in quick, fierce accents. "I will accept all your fancies, and humor all your caprices. I will grant that you do not love me—I will even suppose that I am repellent to you,—but that shall make no difference to my desire! You shall be mine!—willing or unwilling! If every kiss I take from your lips be torn from you with reluctance, yet those kisses I will have!—you shall not escape me! You—you, out of all women in the world, I choose. . ."

"As your wife?" said Ziska slowly, her dark eyes gleaming with a strange light as she dexterously withdrew herself from his embrace.

He uttered an impatient exclamation.

"My wife! Dieu! What a banalite! You, with your exquisite, glowing beauty and voluptuous charm, you would be a 'wife'—that tiresome figure-head of utterly dull respectability? You, with your unmatched air of wild grace and freedom, would submit to be tied down in the bonds of marriage,—marriage, which to my thinking and that of many other men of my character, is one of the many curses of this idiotic nineteenth century! No, I offer you love, Ziska!—ideal, passionate love!—the glowing, rapturous dream of ecstasy in which such a thing as marriage would be impossible, the merest vulgar commonplace— almost a profanity."

"I understand!" and the Princess Ziska regarded him intently, her breath coming and going, and a strange smile quivering on her lips. "You would play the part of an Araxes over again!"

He smiled; and with all the audacity of a bold and determined nature, put his arms round her and drew her close up to his breast.

"Yes," he said, "I would play the part of an Araxes over again!"

As he uttered the words, an indescribable sensation of horror seized him—a mist darkened his sight, his blood grew cold, and a tremor shook him from head to foot. The fair woman's face that was lifted so close to his own seemed spectral and far off; and for a fleeting moment her very beauty grew into something like hideousness, as if the strange effect of the picture he had painted of her was now becoming actual and apparent—namely, the face of death looking through the mask of life. Yet he did not loosen his arms from about her waist; on the contrary he clasped her even more closely, and kept his eyes fixed upon her with such pertinacity that it seemed as if he expected her to vanish from his sight while he still held her.

"To play the part of an Araxes aright," she murmured then in slow and dulcet accents, "you would need to be cruel and remorseless, and sacrifice my life—or any woman's life—to your own clamorous and selfish passion. But you,—Armand Gervase,—educated, civilized, intellectual, and totally unlike the barbaric Araxes, could not do that, could you? The progress of the world, the increasing intelligence of humanity, the coming of the Christ, these things are surely of some weight with you, are they not? Or are you made of the same savage and impenitent stuff as composed the once famous yet brutal warrior of old time? Do you admire the character and spirit of Araxes?—he who, if history reports him truly, would snatch a woman's life as though it were a wayside flower, crush out all its sweetness and delicacy, and then fling it into the dust withered and dead? Do you think that because a man is strong and famous, he has a right to the love of woman?—a charter to destroy her as he pleases? If you remember the story I told you, Araxes murdered with his own hand Ziska-Charmazel the woman who loved him."

"He had perhaps grown weary of her," said Gervase, speaking with an effort, and still studying the exquisite loveliness of the bewitching face that was so close to his own, like a man in a dream.

At this she laughed, and laid her two hands on his shoulders with a close and clinging clasp which thrilled him strangely.

"Ah, there is the difficulty!" she said.

"What cure shall ever be found for love-weariness? Men are all like children—they tire of their toys; hence the frequent trouble and discomfort of marriage. They grow weary of the same face, the same caressing arms, the same faithful heart! You, for instance, would grow weary of me!"

"I think not," answered Gervase. And now the vague sense of uncertainty and pain which had distressed him passed away, leaving him fully self-possessed once more. "I think you are one of those exceptional women whom a man never grows weary of: like a Cleopatra, or any other old-world enchantress, you fascinate with a look, you fasten with a touch, and you have a singular freshness and wild attraction about you which makes you unlike any other of your sex. I know well enough that I shall never get the memory of you out of my brain; your face will haunt me till I die!"

"And after death?" she queried, half-closing her eyes, and regarding him languorously through her silky black lashes.

"Ah, ma belle, after that there is nothing to be done even in the way of love. Tout est fini! Considering the brevity of life and the absolute certainty of death, I think that the men and women who are so foolish as to miss any opportunities of enjoyment while they are alive deserve more punishment than those who take all they can get, even in the line of what is called wickedness. Wickedness is a curious thing: it takes different shapes in different lands, and what is called 'wicked' here, is virtue in, let us say, the Fiji Islands. There is really no strict rule of conduct in the world, no fixed law of morality."

"There is honor!" said the Princess, slowly;—"A code which even savages recognize."

He was silent. For a moment he seemed to hesitate; but his indecision soon passed. His face flushed, and anon grew pale, as closing his arms more victoriously round the fair woman who just then appeared voluntarily to yield to his embrace, he bent down and whispered a few words in the tiny ear, white and delicate as a shell, which was half-hidden by the rich loose clusters of her luxuriant hair. She heard, and smiled; and her eyes flashed with a singular ferocity which he did not see, otherwise it might have startled him.

"I will answer you to-morrow," she said. "Be patient till then."

And as she spoke, she released herself determinedly from the clasp of his arms and withdrew to a little distance, looking at him with a fixed and searching scrutiny.

"Do not preach patience to me!" he exclaimed with a laugh. "I never had that virtue, and I certainly cannot begin to cultivate it now."

"Had you ever any virtues?" she asked in a playful tone of something like satire.

He shrugged his shoulders.

"I do not know what you consider virtues," he answered lightly: "If honesty is one, I have that. I make no pretence to be what I am not. I would not pass off somebody else's picture as my own, for instance. But I cannot sham to be moral. I could not possibly love a woman without wanting her all to myself, and I have not the slightest belief in the sanctimonious humbug of a man who plays the Platonic lover only. But I don't cheat, and I don't lie. I am what I am. . ."

"A man!" said Ziska, a lurid and vindictive light dilating and firing her wonderful eyes. "A man!—the essence of all that is evil, the possibility of all that is good! But the essence is strong and works; the possibility is a dream which dissolves in the dreaming!"

"Yes, you are right, ma chere!" he responded carelessly. "Goodness—as the world understands goodness—never makes a career for itself worth anything. Even Christ, who has figured as a symbol of goodness for eighteen hundred years, was not devoid of the sin of ambition: He wanted to reign over all Judaea."

"You view Him in that light?" inquired Ziska with a keen look. "And as man only?"

"Why, of course! The idea of an incarnate God has long ago been discarded by all reasoning thinkers."

"And what of an incarnate devil?" pursued Ziska, her breath coming and going quickly.

"As impossible as the other fancy!" he responded almost gayly. "There are no gods and no devils, ma belle! The world is ruled by ourselves alone, and it behoves us to make the best of it. How will you give me my answer to-morrow? When shall I see you? Speak low and quickly,—Dr. Dean is coming in here from the garden: when—when?"

"I will send for you," she answered.

"At what hour?"

"The moon rises at ten. And at ten my messenger shall come for you."

"A trustworthy messenger, I hope? One who knows how to be silent?"

"As silent as the grave!" she said, looking at him fixedly. "As secret as the Great Pyramid and the hidden tomb of Araxes!"

And smiling, she turned to greet Dr. Dean, who just then entered the saloon.

"Denzil has gone to bed," he announced. "He begged me to excuse him to you, Princess. I think the boy is feverish. Egypt doesn't agree with him."

"I am sorry he is ill," said the Princess with a charming air of sympathy.

"Oh, he isn't exactly ill," returned the Doctor, looking sharply at her beautiful face as he spoke. "He is simply unnerved and restless. I am a little anxious about him. I think he ought to go back to England—or Scotland."

"I think so, too," agreed Gervase. "And Mademoiselle Helen with him."

MARIE CORELLI

"Mademoiselle Helen you consider very beautiful?" murmured the Princess, unfurling her fan and waving it indolently to and fro.

"No, not beautiful," answered the Doctor quickly. "But very pretty, sweet and lovable—and good."

"Ah then, of course some one will break her heart!" said the Princess calmly. "That is what always happens to good women."

And she smiled as she saw Gervase flush, half with anger, half with shame. The little Doctor rubbed his nose crossly.

"Not always, Princess," he said. "Sometimes it does; in fact pretty often. It is an unfortunate truth that virtue is seldom rewarded in this world. Virtue in a woman nowadays—"

"Means no lovers and no fun!" said Gervase gayly. "And the possibility of a highly decorous marriage with a curate or a bankclerk, followed by the pleasing result of a family of little curates or little bank-clerks. It is not a dazzling prospect!"

The Doctor smiled grimly; then after a wavering moment of indecision, broke out into a chuckling laugh.

"You have an odd way of putting things," he said. "But I'm afraid you may be right in your estimate of the position. Quite as many women are as miserably sacrificed on the altar of virtue as of vice. It is 'a mad world,' as Shakespeare says. I hope the next life we pass into after this one will at least be sane."

"Well, if you believe in Heaven, you have Testament authority for the fact that there will be 'neither marriage nor giving in marriage' there, at any rate," laughed Gervase. "And if we wish to follow that text out truly in our present state of existence and become 'as the angels of God' we ought at once to abolish matrimony."

"Have done! Have done!" exclaimed the Doctor, still smiling, however, notwithstanding his protest. "You Southern Frenchmen are half barbarians,—you have neither religion nor morality."

"Dieu merci!" said Gervase, irreverently; then turning to the Princess Ziska, he bowed low and with a courtly grace over the hand she extended towards him in farewell. "Good-night, Princess!"—then in a whisper he added: "To-morrow I shall await your summons."

"It will come without fail, never fear!" she answered in equally soft tones. "I hope it may find you ready."

He raised his eyes and gave her one long, lingering, passionate look; then with another "Good-night," which included Dr. Dean, left the room. The Doctor lingered a moment, studying the face and form of the Princess with a curiously inquisitive air; while she in her turn confronted him haughtily, and with a touch of defiance in her aspect.

"Well," said the savant presently, after a pause: "Now you have got him, what are you going to do with him?"

She smiled coldly, but answered nothing.

"You need not flash your beautiful eyes at me in that eminently unpleasant fashion," pursued the Doctor, easily. "You see I Know You, and I am not afraid of you. I only make a stand against you in one respect: you shall not kill the boy Denzil."

"He is nothing to me!" she said, with a gesture of contempt.

"I know he is nothing to you; but you are something to him. He does not recognize your nature as I do. I must get him out of the reach of your spell—"

"You need not trouble yourself," she interrupted him, a sombre melancholy darkening her face; "I shall be gone to-morrow."

"Gone altogether?" inquired the Doctor calmly and without surprise,—"Not to come back?"

"Not in this present generation!" she answered.

Still Dr. Dean evinced no surprise.

"Then you will have satisfied yourself?" he asked.

She bent her head.

"For the time being—yes! I shall have satisfied myself."

There followed a silence, during which the little Doctor looked at his beautiful companion with all the meditative interest of a scientist engaged in working out some intricate and deeply interesting problem.

"I suppose I may not inquire how you propose to obtain this satisfaction?" he said.

"You may inquire, but you will not be answered!" she retorted, smiling darkly.

"Your intentions are pitiless?"

Still smiling, she said not a word.

"You are impenitent?"

She remained silent.

"And, worst of all, you do not desire redemption! You are one of those who forever and ever cry, 'Evil, be thou my good!' Thus for you, Christ died in vain!"

A faint tremor ran through her, but she was still mute.

"So you and creatures like you, must have their way in the world until the end," concluded the Doctor, thoughtfully. "And if all the philosophers that ever lived were to pronounce you what you are, they would be disbelieved and condemned as madmen! Well, Princess, I am glad I have never at any time crossed your path till now, or given you cause of offence against me. We part friends, I trust? Good-night! Farewell!"

She held out her hand. He hesitated before taking it.

"Are you afraid?" she queried coldly. "It will not harm you!"

"I am afraid of nothing," he said, at once clasping the white taper fingers in his own, "except a bad conscience."

"That will never trouble you!" and the Princess looked at him full and steadily. "There are no dark corners in your life—no mean side-alleys and trap-holes of deceit; you have walked on the open and straight road. You are a good man and a wise one. But though you, in your knowledge of spiritual things, recognize me for what I am, take my advice and be silent on the matter. The world would never believe the truth, even if you told it, for the time is not yet ripe for men and women to recognize the avengers of their wicked deeds. They are kept purposely in the dark lest the light should kill!"

And with her sombre eyes darkening, yet glowing with the inward fire that always smouldered in their dazzling depths, she saluted him gravely and gracefully, watching him to the last as he slowly withdrew.

XV

The next day broke with a bright, hot glare over the wide desert, and the sky in its cloudless burning blue had more than its usual appearance of limitless and awful immensity. The Sphinx and the Pyramids alone gave a shadow and a substance to the dazzling and transparent air,—all the rest of the visible landscape seemed naught save a far-stretching ocean of glittering sand, scorched by the blazing sun. Dr. Maxwell Dean rose early and went down to the hotel breakfast in a somewhat depressed frame of mind; he had slept badly, and his dreams had been unpleasant, when not actually ghastly, and he was considerably relieved, though he could not have told why, when he saw his young friend Denzil Murray, seated at the breakfast table, apparently enjoying an excellent meal.

"Hullo, Denzil!" he exclaimed cheerily, "I hardly expected you down yet. Are you better?"

"Thanks, I am perfectly well," said Denzil, with a careless air. "I thought I would breakfast early in order to drive into Cairo before the day gets too sultry."

"Into Cairo!" echoed the Doctor. "Why, aren't you going to stay here a few days?"

"No, not exactly," answered Denzil, stirring his coffee quickly and beginning to swallow it in large gulps. "I shall be back to-night, though. I'm only going just to see my sister and tell her to prepare for our journey home. I shan't be absent more than a few hours."

"I thought you might possibly like to go a little further up the Nile?" suggested the Doctor.

"Oh, no, I've had enough of it! You see, when a man proposes to a woman and gets refused, he can't keep on dangling round that woman as if he thought it possible she might change her mind." And he forced a smile. "I've got an appointment with Gervase to-morrow morning, and I must come back to-night in order to keep it—but after that I'm off."

"An appointment with Gervase?" repeated the Doctor, slowly. "What sort of an appointment?"

Denzil avoided his keen look.

"Really, Doctor, you are getting awfully inquisitive!" he exclaimed with a hard laugh. "You want to know altogether too much!"

MARIE CORELLI

"Yes, I always do; it is a habit of mine," responded Dr. Dean, calmly. "But in the present case, it doesn't need much perspicuity to fathom your mystery. The dullest clod-hopper will tell you he can see through a millstone when there's a hole in it. And I was always a good hand at putting two and two together and making four out of them. You and Gervase are in love with the same woman; the woman has rejected you and is encouraging Gervase; Gervase, you think, will on this very night be in the position of the accepted lover, for which successful fortune, attending him, you, the rejected one, propose to kill him to-morrow morning if you can, unless he kills you. And you are going to Cairo to get your pistols or whatever weapons you have arranged to fight with, and also to say good-bye to your sister."

Denzil kept his eyes fixed studiously on the table-cloth and made no answer.

"However," continued the Doctor complacently, "you can have it all your own way as far as I am concerned. I never interfere in these sort of matters. I should do no good if I attempted it. Besides, I haven't the slightest anxiety on your behalf—not the slightest. Waiter, some more coffee, please?"

"Upon my word!" exclaimed Denzil, with a fretful laugh, "you are a most extraordinary man, Doctor!"

"I hope I am!" retorted the Doctor. "To be merely ordinary would not suit my line of ambition. This is very excellent coffee"—here he peered into the fresh pot of the fragrant beverage just set before him. "They make it better here than at the Gezireh Palace. Well, Denzil, my boy, when you get into Cairo, give my love to Helen and tell her we'll all go home to the old country together; I, myself, have got quite enough out of Egypt this time to satisfy my fondness for new experiences. And let me assure you, my good fellow, that your proposed duel with Gervase will not come off!"

"It will come off!" said Denzil, with sudden fierceness. "By Heaven, it shall!—it must!"

"More wills than one have the working out of our destinies," answered Dr. Dean with some gravity. "Man is not by any means supreme. He imagines he is, but that is only one of his many little delusions. You think you will have your way; Gervase thinks he will have his way; I think I will have my way; but as a matter of fact there is only one person in this affair whose 'way' will be absolute, and that person is the Princess Ziska. Ce que femme veut Dieu veut."

"She has nothing whatever to do with the matter," declared Denzil.

"Pardon! She has everything to do with it. She is the cause of it and she knows it. And as I have already told you, your proposed fight will not come off." And the little Doctor smiled serenely. "There is your carriage at the door, I suppose. Off with you, my boy!—be off like a whirlwind, and return here armed to the teeth if you like! You have heard the expression 'fighting the air'? That is what you will do tomorrow morning!"

And apparently in the best of all possible humors, Dr. Dean accompanied his young friend to the portico of the hotel and watched him drive off down the stately avenue of palm-trees which now cast their refreshing shade on the entire route from the Pyramids to Cairo. When he had fairly gone, the thoughtful savant surveyed the different tourists who were preparing to ascend the Pyramids under the escort of their Arab guides, regardless of the risks they ran of dislocated arms and broken shoulder-bones,—and in the study of the various odd types thus presented to him, he found himself fairly well amused.

"Protoplasm—mere protoplasm!" he murmured. "The germ of soul has not yet attained to individual consciousness in any one of these strange bipeds. Their thoughts are as jelly,—their reasoning powers in embryo,—their intellectual faculties barely perceptible. Yet they are interesting, viewed in the same light and considered on the same scale as fish or insects merely. As men and women of course they are misnomers,—laughable impossibilities. Well, well!—in the space of two or three thousand years, the protoplasm may start into form out of the void, and the fibres of a conscious Intellectuality may sprout,—but it will have to be in some other phase of existence—certainly not in this one. And now to shut myself up and write my memoranda—for I must not lose a single detail of this singular Egyptian psychic problem. The whole thing I perceive is rounding itself towards completion and catastrophe—but in what way? How will it—how CAN it end?"

And with a meditative frown puckering his brows, Dr. Dean folded his hands behind his back and retired to his own room, from whence he did not emerge all day.

Armand Gervase in the meanwhile was making himself the life and soul of everything at the Mena House Hotel. He struck up an easy acquaintance with several of the visitors staying there,—said pretty things to young women and pleasant things to old,—and in the course of a few hours succeeded in becoming the most popular personage in the place. He accepted invitations to parties, and agreed to share in various' excursions, till he engaged himself for every day in the coming week, and was so gay and gallant and fascinating in manner and bearing that fair ladies lost their hearts to him at a glance, and what amusement or pleasure there was at the Mena House seemed to be doubly enhanced by the mere fact of his presence. In truth Gervase was in a singular mood of elation and excitation; a strong inward triumph possessed him and filled his soul with an imperious pride and sense of conquest which, for the time being, made him feel as though he were a very king of men. There was nothing in his nature of the noble tenderness which makes the lover mentally exalt his beloved as a queen before whom he is content to submit his whole soul in worship; what he realized was merely this: that here was one of the most beautiful and seductive women ever created, in the person of the Princess Ziska, and that he, Gervase, meant to possess that loveliest of women, whatever happened in the near or distant future. Of her, and of the influence of his passion on her personally, he did not stop to think, except with the curiously blind egotism which is the heritage of most men, and which led him to judge that her happiness would in some way or other be enhanced by his brief and fickle love. For, as a rule, men do not understand love. They understand desire, amounting sometimes to merciless covetousness for what they cannot get,—this is a leading natural characteristic of the masculine nature—but Love—love that endures silently and faithfully through the stress of trouble and the passing of years—love which sacrifices everything to the beloved and never changes or falters,—this is a divine passion which seldom or never sanctifies and inspires the life of a man. Women are not made of such base material; their love invariably springs first from the Ideal, not the Sensual, and if afterwards it develops into the sensual, it is through the rough and coarsening touch of man alone.

Throughout the entire day the Princess Ziska herself never left her private apartments, and towards late afternoon Gervase began to feel the hours drag along with unconscionable slowness and monotony. Never did the sun seem so slow in sinking; never did the night appear so far off. When at last dinner was served in the hotel, both Denzil Murray and Dr. Dean sat next to him at table, and, judging from outward appearances, the most friendly relations existed between all three of them. At the close of the meal, however, Denzil made a sign to Gervase to follow him, and when they had reached a quiet corner, said:

"I am aware of your victory; you have won where I have lost. But you know my intention?"

"Perfectly!" responded Gervase, with a cool smile.

"By Heaven!" went on the younger man, in accents of suppressed fury, "if I yielded to the temptation which besets me when I see you standing there facing me, with your easy and self-satisfied demeanor,— when I know that you mean dishonor where I meant honor,—when you have had the effrontery to confess to me that you only intend to make the Princess Ziska your mistress when I would have made her my wife,—God! I could shoot you dead at this moment!"

Gervase looked at him steadily, still smiling slightly; then gradually the smile died away, leaving his countenance shadowed by an intense melancholy.

"I can quite enter into your feelings, my dear boy!" he said. "And do you know, I'm not sure that it would not be a good thing if you were to shoot me dead! My life is of no particular value to anybody,—certainly not to myself; and I begin to think I've been always more or less of a failure. I have won fame, but I have missed—something—but upon my word, I don't quite know what!"

He sighed heavily, then suddenly held out his hand.

"Denzil, the bitterest foes shake hands before fighting each other to the death, as we propose to do to-morrow; it is a civil custom and hurts no one, I should like to part kindly from you to-night!"

Denzil hesitated; then something stronger than himself made him yield to the impulsive note of strong emotion in his former friend's voice, and the two men's hands met in a momentary silent grasp. Then Denzil turned quickly away.

"To-morrow morning at six," he said, briefly; "close to the Sphinx."

"Good!" responded Gervase. "The Sphinx shall second us both and see fair play. Good-night, Denzil!"

"Good-night!" responded Denzil, coldly, as he moved on and disappeared.

A slight shiver ran through Gervase's blood as he watched him depart.

"Odd that I should imagine I have seen the last of him!" he murmured. "There are strange portents in the air of the desert, I suppose! Is he going to his death? Or am I going to mine?"

Again the cold tremor shook him, and combating with his uneasy sensations, he went to his own apartment, there to await the expected summons of the Princess. No triumph filled him now; no sense of joy elated him; a vague fear and dull foreboding were all the emotions he was conscious of. Even his impatient desire of love had cooled, and he watched the darkening of night over the desert, and the stars shining out one by one in the black azure of the heavens, with a gradually deepening depression. A dreamy sense stole over him of remoteness or detachment from all visible things, as though he were suddenly and mysteriously separated from the rest of humankind by an invisible force which he was powerless to resist. He was still lost in this vague half-torpor or semi-conscious reverie, when a light tap startled him back to the realization of earth and his earthly surroundings. In response to his "Entrez!" the tall Nubian, whom he had seen in Cairo as the guardian of the Princess's household, appeared, his repulsive features looking, if anything, more ghastly and hideous than ever.

"Madame la Princesse demande votre presence!" said this unlovely attendant of one of the fairest of women. "Suivez-moi!"

Without a moment's hesitation or loss of time, Gervase obeyed, and allowing his guide to precede him at a little distance, followed him through the corridors of the hotel, out at the hall door and beyond, through the garden. A clock struck ten as they passed into the warm evening air, and the mellow rays of the moon were beginning to whiten the sides of the Great Pyramid. A few of the people staying in the hotel were lounging about, but these paid no particular heed to Gervase or his companion. At about two hundred yards from the entrance of the Mena House, the Nubian stopped and waited till Gervase came up with him.

"Madame la Princesse vous aime, Monsieur Gervase!" he said, with a sarcastic grin. "Mais,—elle veut que l'Amour soit toujours aveugle! oui, toujours! C'est le destin qui vous appelle,—il faut soumettre! L'Amour sans yeux! oui!—en fin,—comme ca!"

And before Gervase could utter a word of protest, or demand the meaning of this strange proceeding, his arms was suddenly seized and pinioned behind his back, his mouth gagged, and his eyes blindfolded.

"Maintenant," continued the Nubian. "Nous irons ensemble!"

Choked and mad with rage, Gervase for a few moments struggled furiously as well as he was able with his powerful captor. All sorts of ideas surged in his brain: the Princess Ziska might, with all her beauty and fascination, be nothing but the ruler of a band of robbers and murderers—who could tell? Yet reason did not wholly desert him in extremity, for even while he tried to fight for his liberty he remembered that there was no good to be gained out of taking him prisoner; he had neither money nor valuables—nothing which could excite the cupidity of even a starving Bedouin. As this thought crossed his brain, he ceased his struggles abruptly, and stood still, panting for breath, when suddenly a sound of singing floated towards him:

> *"Oh, for the pure cold heart of the Lotus-Lily!*
> *A star above*
> *Is its only love,*
> *And one brief sigh of its scented breath*
> *Is all it will ever know of Death!*
> *Oh, for the passionless heart of the Lotus-Lily!"*

He listened, and all power of resistance ebbed slowly away from him; he became perfectly passive—almost apathetic—and yielding to the somewhat rough handling of his guide, allowed himself to be urged with silent rapidity onward over the thick sand, till he presently became conscious that he was leaving the fresh open air and entering a building of some sort, for his feet pressed hard earth and stone instead of sand. All at once he was forcibly brought to a standstill, and a heavy rolling noise and clang, like distant muttered thunder, resounded in his ears, followed by dead silence. Then his arm was closely grasped again, and he was led on, on and on, along what seemed to be an interminable distance, for not a glimmer of light could be seen under the tight folds of the bandage across his eyes. Presently the earth shook under him,—some heavy substance was moved, and there was another booming thunderous noise, accompanied by the falling of chains.

"C'est l'escalier de Madame la Princesse!" said the Nubian. "Pres de la chambre nuptiale! Descendez! Vite!"

Down—down! Resistance was useless, even had he cared to resist, for he felt as though twenty pairs of hands instead of one were pushing him violently on all sides; down, still down he went, dumb, blind and helpless, till at last he was allowed to stop and breathe. His arms were released, the bandage was taken from his eyes, the gag from his mouth— he was free! Free—yes! but where? Thick darkness encompassed him; he stretched out his hands in the murky atmosphere and felt nothing.

"Ziska!" he cried.

The name sprang up against the silence and struck out numberless echoes, and with the echoes came a shuddering sigh, that was not of them, whispering:

"Charmazel!"

Gervase heard it, and a deadly fear, born of the supernatural, possessed him.

"Ziska! Ziska!" he called again wildly.

"Charmazel!" answered the penetrating unknown voice; and as it thrilled upon the air like a sob of pain, a dim light began to shine through the gloom, waveringly at first, then more steadily, till it gradually spread wide, illuminating with a pale and spectral light the place in which he found himself,—a place more weird and wondrous than any mystic scene in dream-land. He stumbled forward giddily, utterly bewildered, staring about him like a man in delirium, and speechless with mingled horror and amazement. He was alone—utterly alone in a vast square chamber, the walls and roof of which were thickly patterned and glistening with gold. Squares of gold were set in the very pavement on which he trod, and at the furthest end of the chamber, a magnificent sarcophagus of solid gold, encrusted with thousands upon thousands of jewels, which were set upon it in marvellous and fantastic devices, glittered and flashed with the hues of living fire. Golden cups, golden vases, a golden suit of armor, bracelets and chains of gold intermixed with gems, were heaped up against the walls and scattered on the floor; and a round shield of ivory inlaid with gold, together with a sword in a jewelled sheath, were placed in an upright position against the head of the sarcophagus, from whence all the spectral and mysterious light seemed to emerge. With thickly beating heart and faltering pulses Gervase still advanced, gazing half entranced, half terrified at the extraordinary and sumptuous splendor surrounding him, muttering almost unconsciously as he moved along:

"A king's sepulchre,—a warrior's tomb! How came I here?—and why? Is this a trysting-place for love as well as death?—and will she come to me? . . ."

He recoiled suddenly with a violent start, for there, like a strange Spirit of Evil risen from the ground, leaning against the great gold sarcophagus, her exquisite form scarcely concealed by the misty white of her draperies, her dark hair hanging like a cloud over her shoulders, and her black eyes aflame with wrath, menace and passion, stood the mysterious Ziska!

XVI

S tricken dumb with a ghastly supernatural terror which far exceeded any ordinary sense of fear, he gazed at her, spellbound, his blood freezing, his very limbs stiffening, for now—now she looked like the picture he had painted of her; and Death—Death, livid, tortured and horrible, stared at him skull-wise from the transparent covering of her exquisitely tinted seeming-human flesh. Larger and brighter and wilder grew her eyes as she fixed them on him, and her voice rang through the silence with an unearthly resonance as she spoke and said:

"Welcome, my lover, to this abode of love! Welcome to these arms, for whose embraces your covetous soul has thirsted unappeased! Take all of me, for I am yours!—aye, so truly yours that you can never escape me!—never separate from me—no! not through a thousand thousand centuries! Life of my life! Soul of my soul! Possess me, as I possess you!—for our two unrepenting spirits form a dual flame in Hell which must burn on and on to all eternity! Leap to my arms, master and lord,—king and conqueror! Here, here!" and she smote her white arms against her whiter bosom. "Take all your fill of burning wickedness—of cursed joy! and then—sleep! as you have slept before, these many thousand years!"

Still mute and aghast he stared at her; his senses swam, his brain reeled, and then slowly, like the lifting of a curtain on the last scene of a dire tragedy, a lightning thought, a scorching memory, sprang into his mind and overwhelmed him like a rolling wave that brings death in its track. With a fierce oath he rushed towards her, and seized her hands in his—hands cold as ice and clammy as with the dews of the grave.

"Ziska! Woman! Devil! Speak before you drive me to madness! What passion moves you thus—what mystic fooling? Into what place have I been decoyed at your bidding? Why am I brought hither? Speak, speak!—or I shall murder you!"

"Nay!" she said, and her slight swaying form dilated and grew till she seemed to rise up from the very ground and to tower above him like an enraged demon evoked from mist or flame. "You have done that once! To murder me twice is beyond your power!" And as she spoke her hands slipped from his like the hands of a corpse newly dead. "Never again can you hurl forth my anguished soul unprepared to the outer darkness of things invisible; never again! For I am free!—free with an immortal freedom—free to work out repentance or revenge,—even as Man is free to shape his course for good or evil. He chooses evil; I choose revenge! What place is this, you ask?" and with a majestic gliding motion she advanced a little and pointed upward to the sparkling gold-patterned roof. "Above us, the Great Pyramid lifts its summit to the stars; and here below,—here where you will presently lie, my lover and lord, asleep in the delicate bosom of love—here. . ."

She paused, and a low laugh broke from her lips; then she added slowly and impressively:

"Here is the tomb of Araxes!"

As she spoke, a creeping sense of coldness and horror stole into his veins like the approach of death,—the strange impressions he had felt, the haunting and confusing memory he had always had of her face and voice, the supernatural theories he had lately heard discussed, all rushed at once upon his mind, and he uttered a loud involuntary cry.

"My God! What frenzy is this! A woman's vain trick!—a fool's mad scheme! What is Araxes to me?—or I to Araxes?"

"Everything!" replied Ziska, the vindictive demon light in her eyes blazing with a truly frightful intensity. "Inasmuch as ye are one and the same! The same dark soul of sin—unpurged, uncleansed through ages of eternal fire! Sensualist! Voluptuary! Accursed spirit of the man I loved, come forth from the present Seeming-of-things! Come forth and cling to me! Cling!—for the whole forces of a million universes shall not separate us! O Eternal Spirits of the Dead!" and she lifted her ghostly white arms with a wild gesture. "Rend ye the veil! Declare to the infidel and unbeliever the truth of the life beyond death; the life wherein ye and I dwell and work, clamoring for late justice!"

Here she sprang forward and caught the arm of Gervase with all the fierce eagerness of some ravenous bird of prey; and as she did so he knew her grasp meant death.

"Remember the days of old, Araxes! Look back, look back from the present to the past, and remember the crimes that are still unavenged! Remember the love sought and won!—remember the broken heart!—remember the ruined life! Remember the triumphs of war!—the glories of conquest! Remember the lust of ambition!—the treachery!—the slaughter!—the blasphemies against high Heaven! Remember the night of the Feast of Osiris—the Feast of the Sun! Remember how Ziska-Charmazel awaited her lover, singing alone for joy, in blind faith and blinder love, his favorite song of the Lotus-Lily! The moon was high, as it is now!—the stars glittered above the Pyramids, as they glitter now!—in the palace there was the sound of music and triumph and laughter, and a whisper on the air of the fickle heart and changeful mood of Araxes; of another face which charmed him, though less fair than that of Ziska-Charmazel! Remember, remember!" and she clung closer and closer as he staggered backward half suffocated by his own emotions and the horror of her touch. "Remember the fierce word!— the quick and murderous blow!—the plunge of the jewelled knife up to the hilt in the passionate white bosom of Charmazel!—the lonely anguish in which she died! Died,—but to live again and pursue her murderer!—to track him down to his grave wherein the king strewed gold, and devils strewed curses!—down, down to the end of all his glory and conquest into the silence of yon gold-encrusted clay! And out of silence again into sound and light and fire, ever pursuing, I have followed—followed through a thousand phases of existence!—and I will follow still through limitless space and endless time, till the great Maker of this terrible wheel of life Himself shall say, 'Stop! Here ends even the law of vengeance!' Oh, for ten thousand centuries more in which to work my passion and prove my wrong! All the treasure of love despised!—all the hope of a life betrayed!—all the salvation of heaven denied! Tremble, Soul of Araxes!—for hate is eternal, as love is eternal!—the veil is down, and Memory stings!"

She turned her face, now spectral and pallid as a waning moon, up to him; her form grew thin and skeleton-like, while still retaining the transparent outline of its beauty; and he realized at last that no creature of flesh and blood was this that clung to him, but some mysterious bodiless horror of the Supernatural, unguessed at by the outer world of men! The dews of death stood thick on his forehead; there was a straining agony at his heart, and his breath came in quick convulsive gasps; but worse than his physical torture was the overwhelming and convincing truth of the actual existence of the Spiritual Universe, now so suddenly and awfully revealed. What he had all his life denied was now declared a certainty; where he had been deaf and blind, he now heard and saw. Ziska! Ziska-Charmazel! In very truth he knew he remembered her; in very truth he knew he had loved her; in very truth he knew he had murdered her! But another still stranger truth was forcing itself upon him now; and this was, that the old love of the old old days was arising within him in all its strength once more, and that he loved her still! Unreal and terrible as it seemed, it was nevertheless a fact, that as he gazed upon her tortured face, her beautiful anguished eyes, her phantom form, he felt that he would give his own soul to rescue hers and lift her from the coils of vengeance into love again! Her words awoke vibrating pulsations of thought, long dormant in the innermost recesses of his spirit, which, like so many dagger-thrusts, stabbed him with a myriad recollections; and as a disguising cloak may fall from the figure of a friend in a masquerade, so his present-seeming personality dropped from him and no longer had any substance. He recognized himself as Araxes—always the same Soul passing through a myriad changes,— and all the links of his past and present were suddenly welded together in one unbroken chain, stretching over thousands of years, every link of which he was able to count, mark, and recognize. By the dreadful light of that dumb comprehension which flashes on all parting souls at the moment of dissolution, he perceived at last that not the Body but the Spirit is the central secret of life,—not deeds, but thoughts evolve creation. Death? That was a name merely; there was no death,—only a change into some other form of existence. What change—what form would be his now? This thought startled him—roused him,—and once again the low spirit-voice of his long-ago betrayed and murdered love thrilled in his ears:

"Soul of Araxes, cling to my soul!—for this present life is swiftly passing! No more scorn of the Divine can stand whither we are speeding, for the Terrible and Eternal Truth overshadows us and our destinies! Closed are the gates of Heaven,—open wide are the portals of Hell! Enter with me, my lover Araxes!—die as I died, unprepared and alone! Die, and pass out into new life again—such life as mine—such torture as mine—such despair as mine—such hate as mine! . . ."

She ceased abruptly, for he, convinced now of the certainty of Immortality, was suddenly moved to a strange access of courage and resolution. Something sweet and subtle stirred in him,—a sense of power,—a hint of joy, which completely overcame all dread of death. Old love revived, grew stronger in his soul, and his gaze rested on the shadowy form beside him, no longer with horror but with tenderness. She was Ziska-Charmazel,—she had been his love—the dearest portion of his life—once in the far-off time; she had been the fairest of women—and more than fair, she had been faithful! Yes, he remembered that, as he remembered Her! Every curve in her beautiful body had been a joy for him alone; and for him alone her lips, sweet and fresh as rosebuds, had kept their kisses. She had loved him as few women have either heart or strength to love, and he had rewarded her fidelity by death and eternal torment! A struggling cry escaped him, and he stretched out his arms:

"Ziska! Forgive—forgive!"

As he uttered the words, he saw her wan face suddenly change,—all the terror and torture passed from it like a passing cloud,—beautiful as an angel's, it smiled upon him,—the eyes softened and flashed with love, the lips trembled, the spectral form glowed with a living luminance, and a mystic Glory glittered above the dusky hair! Filled with ecstasy at the sight of her wondrous loveliness, he felt nothing of the coldness of death at his heart,—a divine passion inspired him, and with the last effort of his failing strength he strove to gather all the spirit-like beauty of her being into his embrace.

"Love—Love!" he cried. "Not Hate, but Love! Come back out of the darkness, soul of the woman I wronged! Forgive me! Come back to me! Hell or Heaven, what matters it if we are together! Come to me,—come! Love is stronger than Hate!"

Speech failed him; the cold agony of death gripped at his heart and struck him mute, but still he saw the beautiful passionate eyes of a forgiving Love turned gloriously upon him like stars in the black chaos whither he now seemed rushing. Then came a solemn surging sound as of great wings beating on a tempestuous air, and all the light in the tomb was suddenly extinguished. One instant more he stood upright in the thick darkness; then a burning knife seemed plunged into his breast, and he reeled forward and fell, his last hold on life being the consciousness that soft arms were clasping him and drawing him away—away—he knew not whither—and that warm lips, sweet and tender, were closely pressed on his. And presently, out of the heavy gloom came a Voice which said:

"Peace! The old gods are best, and the law is made perfect. A life demands a life. Love's debt must be paid by Love! The woman's soul forgives; the man's repents,—wherefore they are both released from bondage and the memory of sin. Let them go hence, the curse is lifted!"

Once more the wavering ghostly light gave luminance to the splendor of the tomb, and showed where, fallen sideways among the golden treasures and mementoes of the past, lay the dead body of Armand Gervase. Above him gleamed the great jewelled sarcophagus; and within touch of his passive hand was the ivory shield and gold-hilted sword of Araxes. The spectral radiance gleamed, wandered and flitted over all things,—now feebly, now brilliantly,—till finally flashing with a pale glare on the dark dead face, with the proud closed lips and black level brows, it flickered out; and one of the many countless mysteries of the Great Pyramid was again hidden in impenetrable darkness.

VAINLY DENZIL MARRAY WAITED NEXT morning for his rival to appear. He paced up and down impatiently, watching the rosy hues of sunrise spreading over the wide desert and lighting up the massive features of the Sphinx, till as hour after hour passed and still Gervase did not come, he hurried back to the Mena House Hotel, and meeting Dr. Maxwell Dean on the way, to him poured out his rage and perplexity.

"I never thought Gervase was a coward!" he said hotly.

"Nor should you think so now," returned the Doctor, with a grave and preoccupied air. "Whatever his faults, cowardice was not one of them. You see, I speak of him in the past tense. I told you your intended duel would not come off, and I was right. Denzil, I don't think you will ever see either Armand Gervase or the Princess Ziska again."

Denzil started violently.

"What do you mean? The Princess is here,—here in this very house."

"Is she?" and Dr. Dean sighed somewhat impatiently. "Well, let us see!" Then, turning to a passing waiter, he inquired: "Is the Princess Ziska here still?"

"No, sir. She left quite suddenly late last night; going on to Thebes, I believe, sir."

The Doctor looked meaningly at Denzil.

"You hear?"

But Denzil in his turn was interrogating the waiter.

"Is Mr. Gervase in his room?"

"No, sir. He went out about ten o'clock yesterday evening, and I don't think he is coming back. One of the Princess Ziska's servants—the tall Nubian whom you may have noticed, sir—brought a message from him to say that his luggage was to be sent to Paris, and that the money for his bill would be found on his dressing-table. It was all right, of course, but we thought it rather curious."

And glancing deferentially from one to the other of his questioners with a smile, the waiter went on his way.

"They have fled together!" said Denzil then, in choked accents of fury. "By Heaven, if I had guessed the plan already formed in his treacherous mind, I would never have shaken hands with Gervase last night!"

"Oh, you did shake hands?" queried Dr. Dean, meditatively. "Well, there was no harm in that. You were right. You and Gervase will meet no more in this life, believe me! He and the Princess Ziska have undoubtedly, as you say, fled together—but not to Thebes!"

He paused a moment, then laid his hand kindly on Denzil's shoulder.

"Let us go back to Cairo, my boy, and from thence as soon as possible to England. We shall all be better away from this terrible land, where the dead have far more power than the living!"

Denzil stared at him uncomprehendingly.

"You talk in riddles!" he said, irritably. "Do you think I shall let Gervase escape me? I will track him wherever he has gone,—I daresay I shall find him in Paris."

Dr. Dean took one or two slow turns up and down the corridor where they were conversing, then stopping abruptly, looked his young friend full and steadily in the eyes.

"Come, come, Denzil. No more of this folly," he said, gently. "Why should you entertain these ideas of vengeance against Gervase? He has really done you no harm. He was the natural mate of the woman you imagined you loved,—the response to her query,—the other half of her being; and that she was and is his destiny, and he hers, should not excite your envy or hatred. I say you IMAGINED you loved the Princess Ziska,— it was a young man's hot freak of passion for an almost matchless beauty, but no more than that. And if you would be frank with yourself, you know that passion has already cooled. I repeat, you will never see Gervase or the Princess Ziska again in this life; so make the best of it."

"Perhaps you have assisted him to escape me!" said Denzil frigidly.

Dr. Dean smiled.

"That's rather a rough speech, Denzil! But never mind!" he returned. "Your pride is wounded, and you are still sore. Suspect me as you please,— make me out a new Pandarus, if you like—I shall not be offended. But you know—for I have often told you—that I never interfere in love matters. They are too explosive, too vitally dangerous; outsiders ought never to meddle with them. And I never do. Come back with me to Cairo. And when we are once more safely established on the solid and unromantic isles of Britain, you will forget all about the Princess Ziska; or if you do remember her, it will only be as a dream in the night, a kind of vague shadow and uncertainty, which will never seriously trouble your mind. You look incredulous. I tell you at your age love is little more than a vision; you must wait a few years yet before it becomes a reality, and then Heaven help you, Denzil!—for you will be a troublesome fellow to deal with! Meanwhile, let us get back to Cairo and see Helen."

Somewhat soothed by the Doctor's good-nature, and a trifle ashamed of his wrath, Denzil yielded, and the evening saw them both back at the Gezireh Palace Hotel, where of course the news of the sudden disappearance of Armand Gervase with the Princess Ziska created the utmost excitement. Helen Murray shivered and grew pale as death when she heard it; lively old Lady Fulkeward simpered and giggled, and declared it was "the most delightful thing she had ever heard of!"—an elopement in the desert was "so exquisitely romantic!" Sir Chetwynd Lyle wrote a conventional and stilted account of it for his paper, and ponderously opined that the immorality of Frenchmen was absolutely beyond any decent journalist's powers of description. Lady Chetwynd Lyle, on the contrary, said that the "scandal" was not the fault of Gervase; it was all "that horrid woman," who had thrown herself at his head. Ross Courtney thought the whole thing was "queer;" and young Lord Fulkeward said there was something about it he didn't quite understand,—something "deep," which his aristocratic quality of intelligence could not fathom. And society talked and gossiped till Paris and London caught the rumor, and the name of the famous French artist, who had so strangely vanished from the scene of his triumphs with a beautiful woman whom no one had ever heard of before, was soon in everybody's mouth. No trace of him or of the Princess Ziska could be discovered; his portmanteau contained no letters or papers,— nothing but a few clothes; his paint-box and easel were sent on to his deserted studio in Paris, and also a blank square of canvas, on which, as Dr. Dean and others knew, had once been the curiously-horrible portrait of the Princess. But that appalling "first sketch" was wiped out and clean gone as though it had never been painted, and Dr. Dean called Denzil's attention to the fact. But Denzil thought nothing of it, as he imagined that Gervase himself had obliterated it before leaving Cairo.

A few of the curious among the gossips went to see the house the Princess had lately occupied, where she had "received" society and managed to shock it as well. It was shut up, and looked as if it had not been inhabited for years. And the gossips said it was "strange, very strange!" and confessed themselves utterly mystified. But the fact remained that Gervase had disappeared and the Princess Ziska with him. "However," said Society, "they can't possibly hide themselves for long. Two such remarkable personalities are bound to appear again somewhere. I daresay we shall come across them in Paris or on the Riviera. The world is much too small for the holding of a secret."

And presently, with the approach of spring, and the gradual break-up of the Cairo "season," Denzil Murray and his sister sailed from Alexandria en route for Venice. Dr. Dean accompanied them; so did the Fulkewards and Ross Courtney. The Chetwynd-Lyles went by a different steamer, "old" Lady Fulkeward being quite too much for the patience of those sweet but still unengaged "girls" Muriel and Dolly. One night when the great ship was speeding swiftly over a calm sea, and Denzil, lost in sorrowful meditation, was gazing out over the trackless ocean with pained and passionate eyes which could see nothing but the witching and exquisite beauty of the Princess Ziska, now possessed and enjoyed by Gervase, Dr. Dean touched him on the arm and said:

"Denzil, have you ever read Shakespeare?"

Denzil started and forced a smile.

"Why, yes, of course!"

"Then you know the lines—

'There are more things in heaven and earth, Horatio,
Than are dreamt of in your philosophy?'

The Princess Ziska was one of those 'things.'"

Denzil regarded him in wonderment.

"What do you mean?"

"Oh, of course, you will think me insane," said the Doctor, resignedly. "People always take refuge in thinking that those who tell them uncomfortable truths are lunatics. You've heard me talk of ghosts?—ghosts that walk and move about us like human beings?—and they are generally very brilliant and clever impersonations of humanity, too—and that nevertheless are NOT human?"

Denzil assented.

"The Princess Ziska was a ghost!" concluded the Doctor, folding his arms very tightly across his chest and nodding defiantly.

"Nonsense!" cried Denzil. "You are mad!"

"Precisely the remark I thought you would make!" and Dr. Dean unfolded his arms again and smiled triumphantly. "Therefore, my dear boy, let us for the future avoid this subject. I know what I know; I can distinguish phantoms from reality, and I am not deceived by appearances. But the world prefers ignorance to knowledge, and even so let it be. Next time I meet a ghost I'll keep my own counsel!" He paused a moment,—then added: "You remember I told you I was hunting down that warrior of old time, Araxes?"

Denzil nodded, a trifle impatiently.

"Well," resumed the Doctor slowly,—"Before we left Egypt I found him! But how I found him, and where, is my secret!"

Society still speaks occasionally of Armand Gervase, and wonders in its feeble way when he will be "tired" of the Egyptian beauty he ran away with, or she of him. Society never thinks very far or cares very much for anything long, but it does certainly expect to see the once famous French artist "turn up" suddenly, either in his old quarters in Paris, or in one or the other of the fashionable resorts of the Riviera. That he should be dead has never occurred to anyone, except perhaps Dr. Maxwell Dean. But Dr. Dean has grown extremely reticent— almost surly; and never answers any questions concerning his Scientific Theory of Ghosts, a work which, when published, created a great deal of excitement, owing to its singularity and novelty of treatment. There was the usual "hee-hawing" from the donkeys in the literary pasture, who fondly imagined their brayings deserved to be considered in the light of serious opinion;—and then after a while the book fell into the hands of scientists only,—men who are beginning to understand the discretion of silence, and to hold their tongues as closely as the Egyptian priests of old did, aware that the great majority of men are never ripe for knowledge. Quite lately Dr. Dean attended two weddings,—one being that of "old" Lady Fulkeward, who has married a very pretty young fellow of five-and-twenty, whose dearest consideration in life is the shape of his shirt-collar; the other, that of Denzil Murray, who has wedded the perfectly well-born, well-bred and virtuous, if somewhat cold-blooded, daughter of his next-door neighbor in the Highlands. Concerning his Egyptian experience he never speaks,—he lives the ordinary life of the Scottish land-owner, looking after his tenantry, considering the crops, preserving the game, and clearing fallen timber;—and if the glowing face of the beautiful Ziska ever floats before his memory, it is only in a vague dream from which he quickly rouses himself with a troubled sigh. His sister Helen has never married. Lord Fulkeward proposed to her but was gently rejected, whereupon the disconsolate young nobleman took a journey to the States and married the daughter of a millionaire oil-merchant instead. Sir Chetwynd Lyle and his pig-faced spouse still thrive and grow fat on the proceeds of the Daily Dial, and there is faint hope that one of their "girls" will wed an aspiring journalist,—a bold adventurer who wants "a share in the paper" somehow, even if he has to marry Muriel or Dolly in order to get it. Ross Courtney is the only man of the party once assembled at the Gezireh Palace Hotel who still goes to Cairo every winter, fascinated thither by an annually recurring dim notion that he may "discover traces" of the lost Armand Gervase and the Princess Ziska. And he frequently accompanies the numerous sight-seers who season after season drive from Cairo to the Pyramids, and take pleasure in staring at the Sphinx with all the impertinence common to pigmies when contemplating greatness. But more riddles than that of the Sphinx are lost in the depths of the sandy desert; and more unsolved problems lie in the recesses of the past than even the restless and inquiring spirit of modern times will ever discover;—and if it should ever chance that in days to come, the secret of the movable floor of the Great Pyramid should be found, and the lost treasures of Egypt brought to light, there will probably be much discussion and marvel concerning the Golden Tomb of Araxes. For the hieroglyphs on the jewelled sarcophagus speak of him thus and say:—

"Araxes was a Man of Might, far exceeding in Strength and Beauty the common sons of men. Great in War, Invincible in Love, he did Excel in Deeds of Courage and of Conquest,—and for whatsoever Sins he did in the secret Weakness of humanity commit, the Gods must judge him. But in all that may befit a Warrior, Amenhotep The King doth give him honor,—and to the Spirits of Darkness and of Light his Soul is here commended to its Rest."

Thus much of the fierce dead hero of old time,—but of the mouldering corpse that lies on the golden floor of the same tomb, its skeleton hand touching, almost grasping, the sword of Araxes, what shall be said? Nothing—since the Old and the New, the Past and the Present, are but as one moment in the countings of eternity, and even with a late repentance Love pardons all.

FINIS

The Devil's Motor: A Fantasy

In the dead midnight, at that supreme moment when the Hours that are past slip away from the grasp of the Hours yet to be, there came rushing between Earth and Heaven the sound of giant wheels,—the glare of great lights,—the stench and the muffled roar of a huge Car, tearing at full speed along the pale line dividing the Darkness from the Dawn.

And he who stood within the Car, steering it straight onward, was clothed in black and crowned with fire; large bat-like wings flared out on either side of him in woven webs of smoke and flame, and his face was white as bleached bone. Like glowing embers his eyes burned in their cavernous sockets, shedding terrific glances through star-strewn space,—and on his thin lips there was a frozen shadow of a smile more cruel than hate,—more deadly than despair.

"On!" he cried—"Still on! On with an endless rush and roar! Over the plains of the world that is gone,—over the heights of the world to come—on, still on! Without pause, without pity, without love, without regret! Follow me, all ye Forces which are destined to work the ruin of Mankind,—follow! On, on, over all beauty, all tenderness, all truth I ride,—I, the Avenger, the Destroyer, the Torturer of Souls, the Arch-enemy of God! The Kingdom of Hell grows wide and deep,—praise be to Man who makes it! I count up my growing possessions in the ever-breeding spawn of human lust and avarice,—I breathe and live and rejoice in the poison-vapours of human Selfishness! The men of these latter days are my food and sustenance,—the women my choice morsels, my dainty delicates! Brute beasts and blind, they snatch at every lie I offer them;—rejecting Eternal Life, they choose Eternal Death,—verily they shall have their reward! Like a blight my Spirit shall encompass them!—and whosoever would scour the air and scorch the earth must run on the straight road of his desire with Me!"

The great Car flashed along with grinding, thunderous wheels, and as it flew, vast Phantom-forms followed it, like rolling clouds jagged with the lightning,—the fairness of the world grew black, and sulphureous flames quenched all sweetness from the air.

The forests dropped like broken reeds,—the mountains crumbled into pits and quarries, the seas and rivers, the lakes and waterfalls dried up into black and muddy waters, and all the land was bereft of beauty. In the place of wholesome green fields and leafy woods, there rose up gigantic cities, built in on every side, and bristling with thousands upon thousands of chimneys belching forth sickening smoke into the overhanging gloom which hid the skies; and the cities were full of a deafening noise and crashing confusion as of ten million hammers beating incessantly—beating away all peace, all solitude, all health, all rest.

On,—on, and into these countless prisons of stone and mortar the Demon of the Car swept vast and ever-hurrying crowds of human beings, with the furious force of a mighty whirlwind sweeping dead leaves into the sea.

"No room to breathe—no time to think—no good to serve!" he cried— "Now shall you forget that God exists! Now shall you all have your own wild way, for Your way is My way! Now shall you resolve yourselves back to an embryo of worms and apes, and none shall rescue you, no, not one! For the Seven Angels of the Judgment Day are sounding their trumpets of terror, and who shall silence their Voices, or stay the thunderings and lightnings, or the great earthquake?

"Hail and fire!—and the trees, and the green grass burnt up and destroyed!—the sun and the moon, the day and the night smitten into one blackness! We will have no more virtues!—no more hopes of Heaven! Honour shall be as a rag on a fool's back, and Gold shall be the pulse of Life! Gold, gold, gold! Fight for it, steal it!—pile it up, hoard it, count it, hug it, eat it, sleep with it, die with it! Lo, I give it to you in millions, packed down and pressed together in full & overflowing measure—I scatter it among you even as a destroying rain!

"Build with it, buy with it, gamble with it, sell your souls and bodies for it,—there are devils enough in Hell to drive all your bargains! Sneer at truth, defeat justice, snatch virtue's mask to cover vice, drug conscience, feed and fatten yourselves with the lusts of animalism till the cancer of sin makes of you a putrefaction and an open sore in the sight of the sun! Come, learn from me such wisdom as shall compass your own destruction! Unto you shall be unlocked the under-mysteries of Nature, and the secrets of the upper air,—you shall bend the lightning to your service, and the lightning shall slay!—you shall hollow out the ground and delve a swift road through it for yourselves in fancied proud security, and the earth shall crumble in upon you as a grave, and the cities you have built shall crush you in their falling!—

you shall seek to bind the winds, and sail the skies, and Death shall wait for you in the clouds, and exult in your downfall! Come, tie your pigmy chariots to the sun, and so be drawn into its flaming vortex of perdition! All Creation shall rejoice to be cleansed from the pollution of your presence, for God hath sworn to give unto Me all who reject Him, and the Hour of the Gift has come!"

STILL FASTER FLEW THE CAR,—red meteors flashed in its course— and the Phantom shapes which followed its flight crowded together in an ever-thickening, ever-darkening multitude, while bright stars were shaken down from heaven like snowflakes whirling in a winter blast. And, mingling with the grinding roar of its wheels came other sounds,—sounds of fierce laughter and loud cursing,—yells and shrieks and groans of torture,—the screams of the suffering, the sobs of the dying,—and as the Fiend drove on with swiftly quickening fury, men and women and little children were trampled down one upon another and killed in their thousands, and the Car was splashed thick with human blood. And He who was clothed in black and crowned with fire, shouted exultingly as He dashed along over massacred heaps of dead nations and the broken remnants of thrones.

"Progress and speed!" he cried—"Rush on, world, with me!—rush on! There is but one End—hasten we to reach it! No halt by the way to gather the flowers of thought,—the fruits of feeling—no pause for a lifting of the eyes to the wide firmament, where millions of spheres, more beautiful than this which men make wretched, sail on their courses like fair ships bound for God's golden harbours! No time to listen to the singing of the birds of hope, the ripple of the sweet waters of refreshment, the murmur of cool grasses waving in the field of peace;—no time, no stop,—no lull for quiet breathing,—on!—for ever on!"

"Up and ride with me all ye who would reach the goal! Come, ye fools of avarice! Come, ye blown and bursting windbags of world's conceit and vain pretension! Come, ye greedy maws of gluttony—ye human pottles of drink,—ye wolves of vice! Come, ye shameless women of lusts and lies and vanities! Come, false hearts and treacherous tongues and painted faces!—come, dear demons all, and ride with me! Come, ye pretenders to holiness—ye thieves of virtue, who give 'charity' to the poor with the right hand, and cheat your neighbour with the left! Come, ye gamblers with a Nation's honour, stake your last throw! Come, all ye morphia-fed vampires and slaves to poison!—grasp at my wheels and cling! On—on—over the fragments of mighty Empires,—over the hearts of kings and queens,—over the lives of the brave, the good and the wise!—trample them all down and crush them into dust and ashes! What shall we do with wisdom, we who have done with God? What with purity?—what with courage? Naught are these but reproach and bitterness—mere obstacles in the road way which leadeth to destruction;—ride them down! On—on! to the destined end!—on with rush and hurry and panting eagerness to reach the only goal—the last of winning-posts—the close of Certainties,—the GRAVE!"

Like a flashing blur of fiery wheels the Car now spun along in the blackness of the night, and the drifting Phantoms round about it were as great grey sails swelling with the angry blast, and sweeping it onward through the dark.

"Pray no more—hope no more—love no more!" cried the Fiend. "Be as the shifting sands, or as the trembling quicksilver—inconstant, capricious,—ever in motion, never at rest! Change—change and revolt! All ye who weary of old things, behold I give you new! Bodies shall be pampered and souls killed for your pleasure;—foulest vices shall be called merely "sensations,"—each to be tried, excused and condemned in turn,—and virtues shall have no more place at all in the scale of feeling! The music of life shall clash into wild discord—the love of home shall be a lost glory,—tenderness for the young, and reverence for the old, shall be the faded sentiments of the past, only fit for a mummer's jest! Change—change and sensation! Roll out your columns of vaporous notoriety, ye printing-presses of the world!—spread wide the fame of the Anarchist and the Courtesan,—mock and revile the spirits of the wise and true,—noise abroad the name of the Murderer, and treat the Poet with derision—give flattery to the rich and scorn to the humble,—teach nothing but the art of lying,—add venom to the tongue of scandal,—dig up the graves of the great, and kill the reputations of the brave and pure!"

"Help nothing on that is noble—nothing that is honest,—nothing that is of God, or for God,—print every lie, grudge every truth, and let your trumpet-note be that of blatant Atheism and Devilry to the end! Set trade against trade,—community against community,—nation against nation,—until with your windy bombast and senseless twaddle you fill your witches' cauldron of mischief and contention to the full! Up and ride with me, ye Plotters against Peace!—ye whose hands are against every man!—there is no time to be lost—up and away with a rush and a roar!—for the Great Star has fallen from Heaven to Earth, and to Him is given the key of the bottomless pit! The pit is open—the gate stands wide—up, and speed on with Me!"

Like lightning now the great Car tore through space—its flaring lamps flashing, its wheels grinding with the sullen noise of a bursting volcano,—and amidst cries and shrieks indescribable, it leaped, as it were, from peak to peak of toppling clouds that towered above and around it like mighty mountains. And presently it seemed as if a thin, pale line of purple fire glimmered afar off, and by this light was seen a monstrous ridge of dense blackness jutting sharply over some vast incalculable depth of horror. On—still on—the Car rushed; and He of the sable robes and flaming crown urged apace its reckless speed with wild shouts of wilder laughter.

"All the world in such haste to die!" he cried. "All the world gone mad with the craze of movement! Up in the air, down on the earth—all turned to whirling, flying, tossing atoms of dust in a storm, and lo, the End! Be patient now, for ye shall never wander again!—be silent now, for prayer and cursing, laughter and tears are done!—let the hoarded gold drop from your grasp—it can purchase nothing yonder! Was it worth while think you,—this rush headlong, to be cast into silence?"

"Was it worth while to leave the sunshine for this dark?—beauty for this decay?—sweet sounds of love and tenderness for this still glow of the eternal flame which is not quenched—this gnawing of the eternal worm whose appetite is never satisfied? Lo, ye have burnt up a world to light Hell with its flame!—but the world shall blossom again like a flower springing from the dust and ye whose soulless lives have been a curse and an outrage on its fairness, shall pace its pleasant paths no more!

"Rejoice, O earth!—rejoice, O sea!—to be freed of the burden of Mankind! Rejoice, O birds, that the hand of the spoiler shall no longer wound or slay!—rejoice, O trees, that the axe of the destroyer shall no more cast ye down!—rejoice, O all ye living creatures of the field and forest, that Treachery no longer stalks the world in man's disguise! Take back thy planet, O great God, cleansed of a pigmy race! Create a new Humanity!—for this is past!"

On—on,—along the black ridge jutting darkly over silent Immensity, with a whirl of fire and roar of thunder the Car flew,—and then—as if for one brief breathing part of a second it paused!

Like a vast Shadow between Earth and Heaven the Demon stood—his bony hand on the steering-wheel—and every point in his flaming crown scintillating with the sparkle of a million stars. Round about him soared and stooped countless terrific Phantom-shapes—some like wrecked ships—some like torn flags of honour—some like mounted warriors—some like throned kings—some like fair women veiled in a mist of tears,—and beneath his bat-like pinions, outstretched to north and south, there glimmered a pale crowd of white faces, upturned wild eyes and imploring hands—all crushed together in a writhing mass of agony! But no sound came from those dumb mouths agape with terror,—all were silent as Death itself, and only the thunderous roar of the Car echoed through space, as after that infinitely brief pause, it dashed furiously onward and down!—down,—down sheer over the edge of that mystic precipice into the fathomless abyss of the Unseen and Unknown!

A THOUSAND LIGHTNINGS LEAPED AFTER it—a thousand crashing echoes vibrated through the Universe with its fall,—one frightful human cry shuddered up to Heaven,—and then—silence.

Gradually, gently, and by faint degrees, a glimmer of pale gold divided the darkness with the wavering rise of dawn—a cool wind parted the air into sweet breaths of fragrance—and in the centre of the awful stillness a scarlet sun rose slowly, fixing the red seal of God on the closed history of a world!

A Note About the Author

Marie Corelli (1855–1924), born Mary Mackay, was a British writer from London, England. Educated at a Parisian convent, she later worked as a pianist before embarking on a literary career. Her first novel, *A Romance of Two Worlds* was published in 1886 and surpassed all expectations. Corelli quickly became one of the most popular fiction writers of her time. Her books featured contrasting themes rooted in religion, science and the supernatural. Some of Corelli's other notable works include *Barabbas: A Dream of the World's Tragedy* (1893) and *The Sorrows of Satan* (1895).

A Note from the Publisher

Spanning many genres, from non-fiction essays to literature classics to children's books and lyric poetry, Mint Edition books showcase the master works of our time in a modern new package. The text is freshly typeset, is clean and easy to read, and features a new note about the author in each volume. Many books also include exclusive new introductory material. Every book boasts a striking new cover, which makes it as appropriate for collecting as it is for gift giving. Mint Edition books are only printed when a reader orders them, so natural resources are not wasted. We're proud that our books are never manufactured in excess and exist only in the exact quantity they need to be read and enjoyed.

Discover more of your favorite classics with Bookfinity™.

- Track your reading with custom book lists.
- Get great book recommendations for your personalized Reader Type.
- Add reviews for your favorite books.
- AND MUCH MORE!

Visit **bookfinity.com** and take the fun Reader Type quiz to get started.

Enjoy our classic and modern companion pairings!